JOY PREBLE

Balzer + Bray
An imprint of HarperCollins *Publishers*

Balzer + Bray is an imprint of HarperCollins Publishers.

Finding Paris
Copyright © 2015 by Joy Preble
www.epicreads.com

Library of Congress Cataloging-in-Publication Data
Preble, Joy.
    Finding Paris / Joy Preble. — First edition.
        pages   cm
    Summary: "When Leo's sister Paris goes missing, she and her new friend
Max must follow Paris's secret notes and clues to find her"— Provided by
publisher.
    ISBN 978-0-06-232130-5 (hardback)
    [1. Runaways—Fiction. 2. Sisters—Fiction. 3. Cyphers—
Fiction. 4. Dating (Social customs)—Fiction. 5. Secrets—Fiction. 6.
Stepfathers—Fiction. 7. Las Vegas (Nev.)—Fiction. 8. Mystery and
detective stories.] I. Title.
PZ7.P90518Fin 2015   2014027513
[Fic]—dc23   CIP
                                                                    AC

15 16 17 18 19   PC/RRDH   10 9 8 7 6 5 4 3 2 1

First Edition

This one is for Jennifer Rofé, who always knows what I should be writing even before I know it myself.

finding Paris

ONE

MY SISTER LEANS OVER ME AS I AM TRYING TO SLEEP.

"Tobias and I broke up," Paris says. "I need pie."

"Go away," I mumble, face half jammed against my pillow. I squint at her in the darkness. "It's late."

"Leo." She lingers on the *o* like an echo. Clicks on my lamp. I turn my head. A sputter of light blinds my left eye. I blink.

Something stabs my hip as I sit up. SAT prep book. Retakes in two weeks. Paris graduated from Las Vegas High a few weeks ago. She does not care about SAT prep.

"I'm studying." I gesture vaguely to the book.

"No you're not. Let's go." She tugs my arm.

"I have work tomorrow." I rub my nose with the back of my hand. I smell like raspberry frozen yogurt from tonight's Yogiberry shift.

"Leo. We broke *up*." My sister lifts her arms with the last word, like one of those preachers on TV. She leaves them raised, fluttering her fingers.

Last year when she broke up with Gunner Skillings—who was nice enough when he wasn't drinking, which wasn't that often—she moped around three days straight, eating dry Puffins and listening to an endless loop of Pearl Jam and R.E.M. and Nine Inch Nails, because who wouldn't be cheered up by that?

Eventually, I made her eat some protein and do her homework and basically get on with things.

"He's a loser," I told her. "You know that."

Now I sit on the edge of my bed and ask, "Which one is Tobias?"

My sister is private about boys until she's sure things will last—which they rarely do. Tobias is supposedly six foot five and works as a trainer at the 24 Hour Fitness in Silverado Ranch. Which is weird because Paris dates boys like Gunner or Cooper Daniels, who has ink under his nails from drawing, chain-smokes Kents, and plays guitar badly and off-key with a garage band that covers the Cure.

Paris grins but says only, "Pretty, right?" thrusting a hair clip at me: tiny flower petals fixed on the flat surface, glossed to a smooth sheen. A dried glop of translucent glue sits at the tip of her index finger.

My sister's an artist. Not like Cooper Daniels and his amateur comic books that will never go anywhere. She sells her stuff at gift shops—clips and necklaces and rings and pins and slicked-up collages of words and fabric and metal. She doesn't make much yet, but she could. Her room is filled with odds and ends that she turns into something.

I make a noncommittal noise, and she fastens the flower to her long auburn hair. In the shadowy amber light, she looks thin and hollow eyed, like she might blow away with the slightest of winds.

"I need pie," she repeats, foot tapping the carpet. "Breakup pie. Adventure pie."

Her face shifts. She presses a hand to her concave belly. "It's true," she says. "I'm sad, Leo."

I let her haul me from bed.

"I need to sleep," I say, but I'm slipping my feet into flip-flops and combing my fingers through my hair, which used to be shoulder length until last month when I chopped most of it off in this short, angled cut, one part sloping almost over my eye. I streaked that piece purple.

My sister—all smooth perfect skin and cotton sun-dress and dark-green eyes with golden flecks—looks at me sharply, brows drawing together. Her lips part, like she's going to say something. Then she presses them shut and taps a finger to the oblong metal charm hanging from a knotted black cord at her clavicle. It says *Dream*. She repurposed the metal pull thingie from some old piece-of-crap purse she found at a thrift shop and etched letters into it.

Her gaze scans my shorts and a ninjas vs. zombies

3

T-shirt. Paris is not a fan of my fashion sense.

She nudges with her shoulder. "Pie. Now. Hurry."

I need to sleep. I need to study.

I need a lot of things, actually: a fun summer (slim chance). An über high SAT score so I can get into Stanford next year (decent chance). The money to pay for it if I do. A life anywhere but here.

But we are sisters. I watch out for her. That's the way it is with us.

We tiptoe through the dark house on the balls of our feet, not even whispering, headed for the back door. Past the bathroom. Down the hall. Through the family room, skirting around the brown recliner and the big leather sofa, into the kitchen. Stupid cat clock ticking loudly over the stove. It meows every half hour, tail swishing. Who invents things like that?

"Where you two going?"

I jump. Tommy Davis. The fresh-start stepfather who moved us to Vegas from LA three years ago. He won the cat clock as a consolation prize at some small-stakes poker tourney off the Strip. Sitting at the kitchen table sipping what smells like bourbon, feet propped on a chair, biker boots still on. Not that he's a biker, but it's not like they check your authenticity before they sell you the boots.

Paris breezes by him. "You know you're sitting in the dark, right?" she says, also breezily. Tommy mopes when he's on a losing streak. Sits in the dark, elbows on the table, holding his head like it might tumble off.

Lately there's a lot of that.

"Wait," he says, voice raspy.

"What?" I say, still moving, then not.

Tommy huffs a breath. Shifts, bringing feet to floor, one heavy boot clomp at a time. He digs in the back pocket of his jeans—cowboy tight even though he's over forty and has the receding hairline to prove it. His bicep flexes under the short sleeve of his T-shirt. He's caught us leaving other times. As far as I know, he hasn't told Mom. What we do while Callie Hollings deals blackjack on the night shift at Vegas Mike's off the Strip is our business.

"Here," he says, pushing a fifty-dollar bill at Paris. "You girls be careful out there. Buncha crazies, you know." Tommy's big on cash—always has a money clip full even when he's mostly broke.

"Thanks," Paris says, not looking at him. But she doesn't take it.

"Mad money," Tommy says. "Just in case." His gaze slides to me and he eases the bill into my hand.

Paris swings the door open, desert heat hitting like a wall.

"Bye now," she says, reaching for my free hand and lacing her fingers through mine.

But Tommy says, "You could hang out here, too. Order pizza or something." He massages the back of his neck with two fingers. "I'm in the mood for a movie."

Tommy likes those old black-and-white movies. The ones where detectives talk in witty banter and wear fedoras and a femme fatale with red lipstick pumps people full of lead from the tiny handgun hidden in her purse.

I almost stop, but Paris says, "Let's go," and we keep on walking.

Someday I will be gone from this house and I'll be at Stanford—my first choice. My only choice—and eventually I will be something, a doctor, or maybe even a surgeon. Surgeons don't hesitate once they've decided what they need to do. You can't stand in front of an anesthetized patient too scared to cut.

"Pie," says Paris, just to me.

"Pie," I tell her, the door slamming behind us.

TWO

EAST OF THE STRIP, A GROUP OF GIRLS IN SHORT, BRIGHTLY COLORED dresses wrapping their skinny bodies like bandages pose in front of the Hard Rock Hotel as we cross Paradise, a naked blow-up man doll hoisted over their heads. Our ancient Mazda chugs noisily behind a stream of yellow taxis and limos and regular cars, too.

"Look," Paris says, pointing, her face half lit by the orangey glow from the dash. The blow-up doll is crowd-surfing—unshapely plastic torso grazing the girls' heads. Something inside me tightens: at the icky peachy-pink of the fake man, at the tightness of the dresses—each girl's long tan legs scissoring from underneath tiny swaths of jewel tones like pairs of spider limbs.

My back is sweating against the Mazda's cheap vinyl seats. It is one thirty in the morning. Prime time. Normally, we would be singing with the radio, but last week it decided it would only play this one country station. Not even AM, which at least we could listen to and mock the crazies on the call-in shows.

Paris slows to watch the blow-up doll's progression, fingers drumming against the steering wheel. Tonight her nails are different colors: thumb and index bloodred, middle finger navy, ring and pinkie a greenish khaki. A thin braid of leather she's studded with tiny sparkling gems snakes up her arm like a vine.

"He needs a hat," she pronounces, meaning the blow-up doll. I don't grace this with a response.

On the sidewalk, a tall guy strides hunched over, wearing a gas mask. We're headed up Harmon. Unless Paris changes her mind, we'll hook a right near the Cosmopolitan. But directions are fluid in Las Vegas. Tomorrow they might blow up the hotel to build a new one.

I'm still holding Tommy's fifty, balled up in my fist. The edges scrape the inside of my palm like a callus. The AC is on full blast, but we've opened the windows so the heat rushes in, too. It's a powerful sensation—my legs goose bumpy with cold air leaking from the vents, my face warm. I reach my arm out, desert wind racing hot over my skin.

"I could make little ones," Paris says. "Necklaces shaped like blow-up dolls," she clarifies, casting a brief look in my direction. "You could pop them with a pin if you got tired of them. Or if they looked like someone you hate."

"Huh," I say. We hit a pothole and the Mazda rears up, bouncing down hard. My arm slams against the not-quite-fully-open window. Tommy's money flies into the night.

"Shit! Stop." I stick my head out, craning around. The raggedy bill lifts in the air, riding the breeze back toward Paradise.

Paris stomps on the gas and we jerk forward, almost rear-ending a Lexus sedan.

"Fuck," I say. "Whatever."

"Mad money," Paris says, maybe trying to sound like Tommy. She does not turn the car around, and I don't ask again.

And then we're laughing and turning onto the Strip, inching down Las Vegas Boulevard, the Paris Hotel to our right, Bellagio across the street, fountains swaying to classical music blasting loud.

"Tobias first asked me out right there," Paris says, flapping her arm across me toward the Flamingo, all purple and orange and neon glitz.

"Seriously?" I ask, but her eyes are on the road so it's impossible to tell. "How do I not know this? You tell me everything."

I bat her hand away and she puts it back on the steering wheel. Paris likes to drive in the classic 10 and 2 position, sitting up straight like an old lady.

"I was with Margo," she goes on. Margo is her friend from school. "Tobias was talking to the valet and drinking an Arnold Palmer. You know how I love Arnold Palmers."

Actually she does—heavy on the lemonade, lighter on the iced tea. The rest is possibly bullshit. Or possibly true. She supposedly went out with Cooper Daniels because he said he liked the tiny rose tattoo on her shoulder.

"Margo knew him from work. When she used to hostess at that IHOP, remember? He was a line cook," Paris says. "For like a few weeks until he got tired of it. I mean, who wouldn't?"

"Who wouldn't?" I echo.

"I mean it, Leo. I thought he was cute."

"I thought he was a trainer at 24 Hour Fitness."

She glances at me now, sticking out her pointy tongue. "He was, after that."

We inch another few feet, stuck behind a Hummer limo. Someone waves a hand from the moonroof on top.

"Guess where we broke up," she asks cheerfully. "I'll give you three chances."

The Hummer lumbers forward. So do we.

"On the phone?"

Paris makes a raspberry sound. "You're not trying, Leonora. You guess. And then we'll get pie. Or fried Twinkies, maybe. That place downtown on Fremont. You know."

"We could go home," I say.

"Pssh." Paris toots the horn. *Beep. Beep.*

I think about the fifty-dollar bill—briefly. I think longer about my savings—stuffed in an ancient pencil bag at the top of my closet where I stash all my old school stuff:

perfect math tests and not-so-perfect paintings and my old report cards like the one from second grade where the teacher had written, *Leonora gets flustered if she doesn't achieve perfection.* As if that was a bad thing.

I have $5,780, bills neatly stacked and rubber-banded. Job money and birthday money and the money Grammy Marie sent me when her sister in Tacoma died—Great-aunt Agnes who I never met but who put me and Paris in her will anyway. Too much to keep at home, but I don't have a bank account anymore. Why? Because my mother was raiding it every time she got low on cash. Which she never did until Tommy. "I'm feeling flush with cash," he likes to say. Flush it down the toilet is more likely.

"Guess again," says Paris, even though I haven't answered. "Where did Tobias and I break up?"

Something about the way she sounds, her voice thick, makes me lift my gaze from the street. In the wash of neon flooding the windows, her cheekbones look sharper, her face more angular.

"What?" I say.

She sighs and we lurch forward another car length. The Hummer is rocking now. A guy, shirtless but wearing a cowboy hat, rises through the moonroof and waves at us, his skin pale under the neon haze. He stares up and over at the giant new Ferris wheel someone's built in the middle of the Strip, bigger even than that one in London. Idiot.

Paris honks the Mazda's tinny horn again. The heat is

pressing in on us, and my face feels sweaty.

Shirtless guy is throwing kisses.

"Toby kept pushing me," Paris says. "You know."

My pulse flickers. I guess she means sex. I don't know why she won't say it out loud. My sister is no puritan about these things.

"So did you?" I look out the window again. Shirtless guy lifts his arms like he's riding a roller coaster.

"Told him to go to hell," she says. "Bye, bye, Toby. That's what you need to do, Leo. That's what you would do, right?"

She says this like I'm the one who was going out with Tobias the jerk.

"Maybe." Or maybe this whole conversation is really about something else.

"Oh screw it," Paris says, loud enough that I jump. "I need pie." She careens the corner at Sands sharp enough to make the tires squeal and heads us back east. "Heartbreak."

Heartbreak is the Heartbreak Hotel Diner. Paris hostesses there two nights a week. Sometimes more. Sometimes she teases her hair like Priscilla Presley.

"We were there last week," I say.

"Best pie," Paris says. "Absolutely."

"Pie House," I say. "Chocolate cream."

"Closes at midnight."

"Gold Coin, then. Apple-berry."

"Heartbreak," she says, voice chirpy even though my

sister is not the chirpy type. Her eyes stay trained on the road. She knows I'll give in. That's what I do.

I wait a few beats, just for show.

"Heartbreak it is," I say.

"We gotta stick together," Paris says, speeding through a yellow light that turns red while we're still in the middle of the intersection.

Only for some reason my stomach knots and I think that maybe she means the opposite. She's signed up for art classes in the fall at CSN, right here in Vegas. Registered a few days before she walked across the stage, spiky purple platform sandals clomping the wooden floor as our mother clapped and cried and Tommy blew an air horn even though they weren't allowed and I snapped pictures from too far away.

"Till you graduate," Paris said a few weeks ago as she clicked the laptop keys, registering online. "One more year." And then she lowered her voice, tightening her gaze on mine. "We could go back to LA now, Leo," she said. "We really could."

I felt something stir—warm and hopeful, like the sun.

Then reality hit: I had senior year left. My teachers knew me—at least as much as they needed to. Mr. Lippman in physics had already promised a stellar rec. After all, I'd aced that class. One more year of straight As and AP classes.

I wasn't going anywhere but our too-small house that was supposed to be temporary. A rental until my mother and Tommy figured out where they wanted to buy.

Sometimes in bed at night, I pretend I can smell the Pacific, its salty scent riding the air currents from the coast.

"If you needed to go, I would take you," Paris continued, looking at me intently. "We could totally do it."

My sister has this grand sense of how the world works. Misguided, but grand.

Me? I am a math-and-science girl. Rules are everything in math and science. One of them is this: life is untidy and ugly. People mess up. Boys named Tobias break up with you because you won't screw them. Or maybe you break up with them because you did. People hurt each other and make mistakes and shatter promises. Even people we love. Not to mention the ones we don't.

Maybe Tobias really is the reason we're driving around in the middle of the night. The reason why my sister's eyes shine fierce and distracted.

It's not like I have a vast resource of experience in these matters. It's not like I can count Buddy Lathrop, who aced every test in our precalc class. We went out twice this year. Both times he ordered a Coke with no ice because "you get more Coke that way," and his eyes, when we were talking, never left my boobs. When he called a third time, I told him I was busy.

And then I think this: I don't care why we're out here. There are worse places to be than driving around in the night, a neon canopy glittering over our heads.

We cross Paradise again, the glitz behind us in the rearview. Sands Avenue becomes East Twain, not the same thing at all.

Paris touches my hand. "What's that?" She points to a long, thin scratch on the underside of my wrist, where I'd nicked myself on the sharp edge of my nightstand the other day.

"Nothing," I say, pulling my wrist away.

"You need a Band-Aid?" Paris pulls a Hello Kitty Band-Aid—she has this thing for goofy Band-Aids—out of the cup holder. "Here."

"Fine," I say. "It's a *scratch*. Here, look. I'm taking the Band-Aid, okay. Love that Hello Kitty." I snatch it from her hand, but I don't unwrap it.

My sister slams the brakes, and we both jolt forward, seat belts tightening. "You know I'd do anything for you," she says. "Well, maybe not work at that yogurt place. Because it's yogurt, you know?"

Over on the sidewalk, a skinny guy in a ball cap and cargo pants lifts his head to the sky and gives the world the finger.

THREE

ELVIS IS GUARDING THE HEARTBREAK HOTEL DINER AS WE CHUG UP.
He's the older, chunkier, gold lamé Elvis—all those fried
peanut butter and banana sandwiches and probably the
drugs having taken their toll. If you're going to build a
twenty-four-hour diner three miles off the Vegas Strip, in
between a Rite Aid Pharmacy and a massage parlor, you'd
think you would go for young Elvis.

I knee open the passenger door, putting my weight into
it. The Mazda, like Elvis, has seen better days.

It is 2:13 a.m.

"Pie!" Paris shouts into the night. She hurtles out, practically flying, and pulls me from the car. "Get a move on!"

"Pie," I say, not shouting. We push through the heat
toward the Heartbreak, my flip-flops smacking the sticky
asphalt, but Paris detours to the Elvis statue. Patting Elvis

on the leg for luck is our tradition, but I'm not in the mood. "You see it every day you work here."

Paris traces her hand down Elvis's leg, ignoring me. She blows him a kiss, multicolored nails drifting up his leg one last time.

"Ick," I say, nudging with my elbow, then walk away and eventually she follows.

Inside, we slip into a red leather booth. "I'm back," my sister announces, stretching her arms wide like she's about to break into song.

She rolls her eyes at her own cheesiness.

We'd found this place last year, after Tommy bought us the Mazda at some auction and we didn't have to share our mother's car anymore. It's not slick, like the theme restaurants on the Strip. It's just this diner that's been here forever and kept adding Elvis memorabilia. Pictures and guitars and fake blue suede shoes in a shadow box on the wall behind the cash register.

Tourists don't come here much. But one of the hostesses walked out mid-shift in April and Paris applied for the job.

Maureen, who works the graveyard shift, shuffles over and slides glasses of water and straws in front of us. She's wearing a pink waitress dress with pockets at the hips that make her look wider than she really is. Also: clunky white lace-up shoes and pink ankle socks. A pencil is tucked behind her left ear. Her lipstick is fire-engine red. Except for the waitress dress, none of it is a required uniform. I admire this on general principle.

"Miss me?" Paris asks, smiling toothily.

Maureen clutches her hands to her chest. Her knuckles are big, like a guy's. "Horribly," she says, rolling her eyes to the ceiling. "I could barely go on." She drags the back of one hand across her forehead, then makes a fake crying sound.

"That's the spirit," says my sister.

They both laugh even though, honestly, I don't find it that funny. But Paris adores Maureen. Says she tells it like it is, which is one of those clichés but I know what she means. "She's a tough one," Paris informs me. "She's been through stuff." My sister has not told me what kind of stuff she means, and I haven't been inspired to ask.

Now Maureen drops the fake drama and tells my sister, "You're on dinner shift tomorrow." She does not ask why we are here at two in the morning. Then again, this is Vegas. Lots of people are lots of places at two in the morning.

She brings us menus and, gesturing to our waters, observes that we look tired and perhaps we should hydrate.

"I broke up with Tobias," Paris announces happily, scooting her straw from its wrapper with her thumb.

Maureen cocks a thin, penciled-in eyebrow. "Good," she says, and she eyes both of us—back and forth until something feels twisty in my stomach because unlike Paris, I don't really know her. But something crashes in the kitchen and she swears under her breath and shambles off.

"What will it be tonight?" Paris asks in her fake formal

voice, drawing out the "be" with a flourish of her hand. "Coconut cream? Peanut butter and banana?"

I decide on coconut cream. Paris pisses me off by not choosing, telling me that she'll eat some of mine. She takes a delicate sip from her water glass. My sister is the effortlessly thin person who can wear cotton sundresses with spaghetti straps and no bra.

I am the more solid type. I do not need the pie.

"So Tobias?" I ask, since she keeps bringing it up. Sometimes my sister has trouble with the truth. Especially when it's personal. "He didn't go to prom with you," I say.

"Because I didn't go," she reminds me. "Prom is antiquated."

But I knew that a vintage seventies dress—sleek, red, sexy—sat in the back of her closet. On the night of her prom, we'd hung out downtown till after three, playing penny slots when no one was checking to see that we were underage, then sharing a Belgian waffle doused with way too much syrup at Du-par's in the Golden Gate.

I didn't ask her why she wasn't at prom, just waited for her to tell me, which she never did. Like when she failed senior English first semester last year because she was staying up making dozens of those gem-and-leather bracelets. A gift shop in the Flamingo had said they'd stock them for her and it was all she could think about. She pulled all-nighters, designing and gluing and then the deal fell through and so did her English grade.

After she confessed what happened, Paris didn't make

another bracelet for almost a month. "I can't," she said. "I mean, why? What's the point?" And what I wanted to say was that it was her passion. That I had nothing I loved as much as she loved art—not even science, which I adored. I played the violin for a year in middle school. In junior high, I played volleyball for a season. But they were not—it turned out—portable passions. We moved and moved and I changed schools and sometimes it was the middle of the year. I was too late for tryouts when we moved here my freshman year.

"Make the damn bracelets," I finally told her one day, sick and tired of watching her mope. "Enough already." As much as I hoped I could someday be a doctor, I knew I wasn't attached to this goal in the same way as my sister was to making pretty things. But I was good at math and biology and chemistry. I dissected frogs and fish and even a fetal pig in biology with no problem. When my counselor sophomore year asked me what I wanted to be, this is what I told her. She nodded sagely and checked it off in my folder.

The idea felt real then, I guess because I'd said it aloud.

After that, things felt better. I joined Mu Alpha Theta and went to math competitions. I made National Honor Society. I was an alternate on the Academic Bowl team and when Zach O'Malley got caught drinking under the bleachers at the football game, I moved up and helped us win the competition in Reno. (Where we snuck vodka into our water bottles in the Holiday Inn.)

Paris pushes from the booth, skips (yes, actually) to the back counter. "Coconut cream," I hear her call into the kitchen.

My gaze drifts over the booths and pictures and what claims to be an authentic Elvis guitar hanging from the ceiling. Below it, smack in the middle of the Heartbreak, elbows on the table, a boy hunches, reading, fingers holding a triangle of club sandwich.

His dark hair is longish—like he forgot to cut it or maybe he's just dead broke. There's a lot of that going around.

He angles his feet under the table. He's wearing khakis and a blue button-down with the sleeves rolled up and worn-looking cowboy boots. My friend, Natalie, would turn up her nose at the boots, but she moved back to New Jersey, so I don't have to remind her that even though we're in Vegas, Nevada's the west and there are cowboys here. Maybe some of them even wear khakis. Natalie was judgmental like that.

Something about the tilt of his chin catches my attention. A strong chin, kind of squarish but in a good way.

Paris strolls back then, sliding the plate between us, the thick slab of pie wiggling, a few tiny shavings of too-brown toasted coconut drifting to the plate.

"Talk to him," she says, and my pulse jolts when I realize she's seen me checking out sandwich/book/cute guy. "I dare you." She leans toward me in the booth. Her voice is suddenly higher pitched. Paris is all about the challenge.

Like life in general isn't good enough without artificially raising the stakes.

Or maybe she just likes to boss me around because she's older.

"You won't, though, Leonora." She uses my full name, fingers drumming an uneven beat on the shiny Formica table.

"Maybe I will," I lie, folding the paper from the straw over and over, a skinny accordion. I poke a finger at the pie. Pinch up a couple coconut shavings. They taste chewy and stale.

Cute boy nibbles his sandwich, head still bent over the textbook. A lock of that longish brown hair falls over his forehead. He brushes it back, but it falls again, and this time he leaves it.

He looks older than me but not by much—eighteen or nineteen, maybe. I am not an artist like my sister, but there is something about the way the light hits the side of his face and his neck as he leans his chin onto the curve of his hand. Like those Renaissance paintings we saw once at the Getty in LA—this museum so high up on a hilltop that you have to take a tram to get up there and when you do, it's all bright white curving buildings and gardens and so much pretty stuff that it almost hurts your heart.

And then my sister says, "He's no Buddy Lathrop," and I feel my face redden. But her voice is soft and I can tell that she means this to be encouraging.

"*You* go if you're so interested," I say, scraping a bit of cream topping with my fork. "You're the one who's on the Tobias rebound, right?"

What is with her tonight? If cute boy senses us staring, he doesn't let on, just bites more sandwich and keeps reading whatever he's reading. His head dips lower, piece of hair still flopping, light angling his face.

Something loosens inside me, which is silly, right? He's a boy who looks good even under fluorescent lighting. That's all. I am not Bella Swan or one of those other girls in those books.

Only here's the thing: I don't want pie. I don't want to talk about Tobias. I don't want to go back home and watch some old detective movie with Tommy Davis whose fifty-dollar bill may still be drifting along Paradise.

I calculate all this briefly. Come up empty because some things have no mathematical answer.

"Okay," I say, and Paris's eyes widen. She grins like an idiot, showing her gums. My sister is a crazy person. I flick my purple-streaked sort-of-bangs with my thumb. Bad idea, this haircut, but these things happen. I slide from the booth. Almost as an afterthought, I take the plate of coconut cream pie with me.

Heart pounding, I saunter to the boy, his head still bent over what I see now is a textbook.

"Pie?" I ask casually, setting the plate on his book. He looks up, blinking. His eyes are gray. Not dark. Not light. Just gray. Ordinary eyes, which relieves me somehow.

"Coconut cream," I say, pulse speeding as he glances at the pie then me. He has a tiny scar over his left eyebrow, thin and white like it's been there awhile.

A drizzle of mayo drips from the wedge of sandwich and trickles down his wrist.

When he still doesn't say anything, I glance at the textbook.

Physics. Okay, that's good.

He's still looking at me, waiting. There's a smudge of escaped mayo on his wrist. I resist the impulse to reach over and wipe it off. He lifts one eyebrow—the one with the tiny white scar cutting through it. His superhero chin angles up, just a little. His jawbones stretch straight and even, with just a hint of stubble.

My breath catches. I can walk away. I should walk away.

But I've already handed him the pie.

"A neutron walks into a bar and asks how much a drink costs," I say, bolder now.

The boy blinks again. One side of his mouth curves up and then he's smiling full-on, bright as the sun. My chest tightens. Any second now, I'll know that the physics book is just a prop to pick up girls in the middle of the night.

"And the bartender replies, 'For you no charge,'" he finishes.

This is how I meet Max Sullivan.

FOUR

"I'M MAX," SAYS MAX. HE'S STILL SMILING.

"You finished my joke," I say, and then, "Leo." I hold out my hand.

"Leonora," I amend, and feel my face ignite because it sounds so bossy, which is not what I had in mind.

Max's lips twitch. I realize with a jolt of stupidity that I've initiated a handshake with someone who's got to drop his bacon and turkey on whole wheat to accommodate me. "Leo Leonora."

"Just Leo," I say, annoyed.

He sets his bite of sandwich on the plate, wipes— finally!—the mayo from his wrist, and pushes back from the table, chair scraping the white tile. He's a lot taller than me. I have to look up to talk to him, and there are those eyes again—those eyes! A medium gray with little blue flecks near the irises. I know this because he's still staring at me. And despite the mayo, I find myself staring back.

Any second now his eyes will do a Buddy Lathrop and stray to my boobs. But Max's eyes do not leave my face.

Then he reaches out and shakes my hand vigorously, like a politician or something—his palm and fingers warm and rough against mine.

"Leo?" he says. This time his voice is a question. "Do you always bring strangers pie?"

I don't think, just say, "Only if they know about neutrons," then as our hands let go, I pivot on my heel, heart pounding, and walk back to Paris, who is smirking and twirling a piece of her long hair around her index finger.

Behind me, I hear boot steps.

Above us, Elvis finishes "Don't Be Cruel" and begins crooning "Love Me Tender."

I turn. Max is right behind me, plate in hand.

He forks a bite, chewing, and licks a strand of coconut from his lip.

"This is Max," I tell Paris. "Max, this is Paris. My sister."

Paris smiles, high wattage. Her pulled-back hair swishes. She studies Max, green-eyed gaze roving his face and then flitting over the rest of him:

Arms and face tan—the kind of tan you get when you're outside a lot. Nice, straight nose. Nice-shaped lips, too. Buddy Lathrop had this thin upper lip that disappeared when we kissed, so that my mouth kept slipping upward and bumping into his nose. Yet another reason that we never went out a third time.

"Paris," Max says. "As in France?" He runs the tines of the fork over the top of the pie, raking up cream filling.

"Exactly," Paris says, smiling again, and I wonder if Max can hear the lie in her voice. "My mother loves France. It's her favorite country. In fact, she loves it so much that I was conceived there. Isn't that right, Leonora?" She turns to me, grinning.

"Yes," I say. "Our family is big on France."

My brain starts churning, thinking what else I might add to this story that is what people expect but not at all the truth, when Max asks, "What about you?" He points at me with the fork, licked clean. In these situations, when I am with my sister, no one usually asks.

"The lion?" Max says. "Someone wanted you to be brave?" He means the Leo part.

Paris clears her throat.

"Bright and shining," I say, which is what *Leonora* means, although right now I feel neither of these. Maybe because this makes me uncomfortable, I swipe the plate from his hand, fork too. I slide into the booth next to Paris and, hoping that he has no communicable diseases, dig into the remains of the coconut cream.

Any second now, Paris is going to decide we need to go home or to the all-night movie theater or maybe over to the Strip or to Fremont Street, to watch the tourists zipline on

SlotZilla, if it's still running this late.

I will follow her, and Max will go back to his physics and his club sandwich and that will be that.

I wait for Paris to make her move. The pie is gone. It's time to go.

But she says instead, "You forgot your book," pointing to Max's table.

There's a pause, and then Max says, "Ah," like Paris has made a philosophical observation or posed a question about thermodynamics or the laws of attraction.

"Be right back," says Max, eyes flickering darker.

In the short seconds, not even thirty, that it takes him to collect his book and leave his sandwich, Paris whispers excitedly, "He's nice, right?"

And I say, "Yeah, I guess," not whispering. I don't even attempt to interpret her enthusiasm.

My sister leans across the table, her silver Dream charm tapping the Formica. "He is," she insists.

"Okay," I say, running my finger through a dot of filling left on the plate. "Sure." Sometimes with Paris it's easier to agree.

"Good, Leo," Paris says. "Good." She pats my arm, crazy multicolored nails bobbing.

Book in hand, Max returns.

Paris slides up and off the red vinyl bench, and I start to do the same, except then she says, "Wallet?" and I realize that I left it in the car because she was rushing me. Paris is the

28

driver's-license-in-her-pocket-let-someone-else-figure-out-how-to-pay type.

More than once she challenged us to spend an entire Saturday with only our spare change and any money we found on the ground. In Vegas, I learned that tourists toss loose change into every fountain they see. We went to the movies, paying with our plastic sack of coins. It was an old game of hers, that.

We'd done it back in Santa Monica, too, at places like this funky old theater called Beach Cinema—partly because we were frequently broke and partly because I think we both secretly worried that maybe things would get worse in our lives and at least we'd be ahead of the game. We went to the movies there a lot in any case. This guy, Oscar, who ran the upstairs lobby bar, would put extra cherries in our Cokes and sometimes we'd stay and watch the movie twice, emerging finally in the late-afternoon sunlight, squinting like moles.

"Gimme the keys," I say, but she scrunches her face and says she'll go, then narrows her eyes at Max and adds, "And don't even offer to pay for our pie. We're not that type of girl."

Actually, sometimes we are, but Max doesn't need to know that.

She sashays off, ponytail bouncing under the flower clip. "Carry on," she calls over her thin shoulder.

Max and I look at each other. The AC is pumping and

the vinyl of the booth seat feels cold and sticky against my bare legs. Maybe, I think now, the ninjas vs. zombies T-shirt is not my strongest look.

"So, Max," I say, then stop. There is really no point in engaging him in further conversation, is there?

But he looks at me expectantly and out of my mouth pops, "So physics?" because he's still holding the book.

"It's my job," he says matter-of-factly.

"Physics is your job?"

"Explaining atom-splitting and nuclear fission to patrons of the medium-famous Atomic Testing Museum."

Is he kidding? I eye him more closely. I have made some mistakes in my life—including those two dates with thin-lipped Buddy Lathrop—but I know when something sounds too perfect to be true.

"The one by the Hard Rock?" We've driven by it like a million times but never gone in.

"The very same." He does not seem surprised that I know this.

"Seriously?"

"Like a heart attack," Max says. "Or like the Bikini Atoll explosion. Take your pick."

He's been standing this whole time, but now he slides into the booth across from me, glancing at his phone and then stuffing it in his pocket. He smiles happily, like talking about atomic bombs jazzes him. "Usually people aren't this excited. They're more like, 'So is it a casino, too? Is there a buffet? Are there slot machines?'"

"It's Vegas," I say, looking at my hands and then not. "I think that's required."

It's a part-time job, he tells me enthusiastically, like he's trying to sell me on the concept. He's taking this year off from college and traveling. Nothing permanent. He leans across the table as he talks, close enough that I can smell his cologne—something lemony and clean. Some guys— they smell good from a distance, but up close the scent is heavy like they're trying to drown you in it.

Max smells nice.

"Vegas isn't permanent for anyone," I say. "Even if it is," I add, thinking about our house and Tommy Davis, who shouldn't be anybody's idea of permanent, only our mother married him anyway.

It was a small wedding—just Mom and Tommy and me and Paris and the justice of the peace who married them. I made Mom's bouquet from wildflowers and tiny burnt-orange tea roses tied with antique lacy white ribbon. Paris loaned her earrings she'd made—dangly ones with blue stones. Tommy wore a brown suit. The week before the ceremony, he tattooed our mother's name, Callie, in script along the inside of his wrist.

Mom and Tommy kissed when it was over, and Paris and I applauded and then we all went out for lunch.

A few days later, Tommy quit his sales job at Best Buy, we packed up everything into a rented U-Haul and drove through the desert to Vegas.

Sometimes I think people do things only because they're afraid of not doing them.

"You want coffee or something?" Max asks. He has just finished telling me about how the gift shop at the museum sells Albert Einstein action figures. Bobbleheads, too.

Which is when I realize Paris has been gone a really long time. How long does it take to go get *my* money?

I tell Max no about the coffee and then there's an awkward silence and my skin prickles—just a little.

"Excuse me," I say, pulse knocking—more than a little. "I, uh, need to see what Paris is up to."

"No worries," Max says, voice cheery. He flicks his thumbnail over a rough spot on the table. Max Sullivan is the happy type, I guess. Except for those gray eyes. They look more serious.

I ease from the booth, feeling silly. Paris is just spacing out by the car. Or Tobias called her while she was outside. Maybe she's getting back with him. Maybe they're fighting over the phone. But my heart is beating faster. I don't have time for this. I really don't. And not just because it has occurred to me that I *like* talking to Max Sullivan.

I walk past Waitress Maureen, trying to look casual— she gives me a "what's up" look, but I keep walking—out the door and into the wall of desert heat, hot as a blast furnace. Behind me, Elvis booms "Jailhouse Rock" on the PA.

I expect to see my sister as I hit the parking lot.

But I don't.

Plus, where's our car? We'd parked in the first row, closest to the door. The row that is now empty. What?

I sprint around the parking lot, sweat beading on the back of my neck. Did I forget where we parked? Not likely. Also, three in the morning is late even for a city that doesn't sleep. There aren't many cars left.

Another lap and I'm sure of it.

Our Mazda is gone.

My stomach knots.

I've been ditched.

Shit. My pulse beats in my ears. Now? *Now* she does this? I knew there was something. . . . Why?

I reach in my pocket for my phone. And remember it's in my car. With my wallet.

Paris has left me at the Heartbreak Hotel Diner in the middle of the night, five miles from home, with approximately thirty cents and a ball of dryer lint in my shorts pocket.

My heart rate rockets to somewhere between pissed off and panic.

I storm back to the diner. Maureen is over by the kitchen, but Max glances up, eyebrows arching.

"I need to use a phone." I force myself to add, "Please?" because even to my ears it sounds like I'm about to bite his head off.

I wait for him to question this or tell me to try Maureen

or ask me why, but Max hands over his cell and doesn't say a word.

I cannot believe she did this to me.

I press in the numbers—my hand is shaking from adrenaline and it takes me two tries before I get it right. The phone rings. And rings. And rings. Her voice mail picks up.

I try it again. A third time.

I text her.

No answer.

I dial again and leave a message.

I think of calling my mother, but I don't. She never answers when she's at work. If she did, she couldn't leave anyway.

We don't have a landline. Can't remember the last time we did. If ever.

I don't call Tommy's cell, either.

"You okay?" Max asks. "Where's your sister?"

"Don't know," I say, and figure that covers it.

If the mysterious ex-boyfriend Toby has a phone, I don't know how to reach it.

"What is it, dollie?" Maureen has plodded over and she pats my shoulder with a thick-fingered hand.

"I don't know," I say, breath sticking, hands clammy. This is totally like her. I shouldn't be surprised. But my heart clatters anyway.

"Where's Paris?" Maureen's lips purse into an *O*, her red lipstick flaking like old paint in the lines. The dangly red-stone earrings Paris made for her bobble against the top of her jaw.

"Gone." I try to say it like it's no big deal. It comes out sounding panicked. Maureen glances over her shoulder at the kitchen, like maybe my sister is going to pop out with a tray of pancakes or something.

She's still looking at the kitchen when she says, "Your sister's a good girl," as though answering a question I haven't asked.

"Yeah," I say. "She's the best."

Maureen frowns, like she's not sure if I'm being sarcastic.

"It'll be all right, Leo," Maureen says in that way people do when they don't want to deal with you.

"You need a ride?" Max hands Maureen a twenty-dollar bill and tells her that this should cover both checks and that she should keep the change.

"You don't have to do that," I say, shoving my hand in my pocket as though money will miraculously materialize. Probably, I realize, Maureen would comp us the pie anyway. But he's already done it.

I don't thank him—I mean, it's not like I asked for it—just push past him.

"Leo." Maureen rests a hand on my shoulder. I shrug it away, stepping back, but she follows me.

"Is he bothering you?" she asks with a narrow-eyed look at Max. Her breath smells like coffee and something fried. "Just say the word and he's out of here."

She'd do it, too. I know she would. Another thing my sister likes about Maureen. She is not the tolerating type.

"It's fine," I say, even though it's not.

She scowls at me. "I see things working this job," she says, as though this explains everything. "I know how people are." She doesn't elaborate.

I feel silly and confused. Max is probably just trying to help. People do that sometimes, right?

I gawk at Maureen for a few beats, then wheel out of reach, head toward the door. Max is still standing there, clutching his textbook.

I have no idea what I plan on doing. I have no money for a taxi. Walk home, I guess. There's a spare key hidden in the bottom of our falling-apart grill on the back patio so that's not a problem. Vegas Mike's is about three miles in the opposite direction. I could go there, too, and wait for Mom.

No big deal. Not the worst thing, I remind myself. Except that when I flip-flop outside, Mr. Physics follows me.

He's just a boy. But my face heats and my heart is hammering and the fact that he's following me makes it hammer faster.

But it's not like I *know* him. Or that I want *him* to know that there really is no one else I can call. Even if I had my phone. My brain runs the short list of people I could call. Marisol from physics, who I studied with before tests. Keesha from Academic Bowl, who Natalie and I had lunch with all of last year. We used to play practice games while we ate our sandwiches. But it's not like they're my friends. It's been me and Paris for so long, the two of us as we moved from place to place to place. Even if I wanted someone else, we were gone too soon. Natalie seemed enough. Until she moved.

Possibly I need to rethink my personal friendship policy.

"Nothing to see here," I say to Max over my shoulder, walking. "Go on. Shoo. I know Krav Maga." This comes out of my mouth sounding not at all like Israeli martial arts—which, in any case, I do not know.

I wince—*Stupid, Leo.* My squinty eye catches a flash of silver on Elvis's leg that wasn't there before.

"I'm not a crazy stalker," Max calls from behind me. "Do crazy stalkers tell physics jokes?" Max Sullivan is clearly the persistent type.

I do not have time for persistent types. My attention is on Elvis's leg.

Written in silver Sharpie on Elvis's chipping white pants leg in familiar, tiny print are these words: *For Your Eyes Only!*

There's a note taped to the leg with a Hello Kitty Band-Aid. It's folded tight and tiny in this intricate pattern my sister likes to use. Like those paper fortune-teller things Paris used to make for us where when you'd open a piece it would tell you things like "He loves you" or "Try again."

My heart is pounding faster than it seems good for a heart to do.

I peel off the Hello Kitty Band-Aid. The note drops into my palm. I unfold it, fingers shaking. I tell myself not to be silly.

In my sister's precise silver script, I see:

Stay calm, Leo. This is the only way.
He's making me. You have to find me.
xParis O OO 1 36

My heart beats its way into my esophagus and lodges there.

"Whoa," says Max. I'd forgotten he was even there.

Our elbows bump as we both bend to read the leg again, and the note—like maybe this time it will say something different. Or nothing at all.

Did she write this because of Tobias? Is she in trouble? Has she run away? My brain fires all the possibilities. None of them stick.

My sister has flaked out on me and left a crazy note telling me to find her. I wheel around again. No Paris. Still.

"What's with the note?" Max is watching me in a way that needs interpretation: Sorry for me, maybe? Or confused? Or just wowed by my personal crisis. I do not have time for analysis.

"She do this a lot?" he asks.

"No. Yes. I— It's Paris," I say, the panic shifting into something darker and more pissed off. "This is the kind of thing she does."

Which it is, sort of. My sister likes to make the world more interesting.

He nods, but I know this is different. Not like last year at a party at her friend Margo's when she decided we should tell everyone we were witches just to see what they would do. (No one cared.)

This feels like something else. But what?

Is she really in trouble? I have to find her.

"You need a ride?" Max asks again. He's staring, head tilted, arms crossed, physics book tucked under his elbow, some strands of slightly-too-long hair curled at the bottom of his neck. I smell the cotton of his shirt, and sweat—just a little—and the vague traces of that lemony cologne.

I do not take rides from boys I do not know. I do not ask for help, period.

But my options are limited. I have no car. No phone. No wallet. It's a long walk in the dark.

Things happen like this, I know. One minute you're whistling along and the next, life has gone off-kilter. The trick is to shift with it, like a computer resetting after an error.

I size up Max Sullivan and decide that he is not Hannibal Lecter.

And when he asks a third time about needing the ride, I acknowledge that maybe I do.

FIVE

MAX SWEEPS ASIDE EMPTY GUM WRAPPERS AND CRUMPLED SACKS from a wide variety of fast-food establishments and tosses a scattered pile of books into the back, chucking the physics book on top. He turns the key in the ignition and the truck—a black Ford Ranger—coughs to life, idling noisily.

"Need a tune-up," Max announces. He chews his lip briefly but looks otherwise unperturbed.

I reach under my ass and extract a laminated name tag on a blue lanyard. *Max Sullivan. Atomic Testing Museum. Las Vegas, Nevada.* In the picture, he's looking off to the side rather than at the camera.

"Here," I say, holding it between two fingers. Max Sullivan is a slob.

He loops the lanyard over the rearview mirror. It swings back and forth in the updraft from the AC.

I can still go back to the Heartbreak and call a cab. When we get to my house, I'll tell him I have to go inside to get cash. Maybe I should do that.

My hip hugs the door—just in case. If time travel existed, I could go back an hour or two and know enough to follow Paris outside. Or go forward and already be home, knowing what was going to happen. Of course in sci-fi stories it never works like that. Someone screws up the future by changing the past and the apes end up in charge or everyone gets stuck in some causality loop—repeating an event over and over but never getting what they want because that's not how it works.

Yes, this is what crosses my mind.

We're still idling in the parking lot.

"Lemme see," Max says, gesturing to the note, and I hand it to him, keeping space between us. There are crumbs of something gummy on the seat. Possibly I will need a tetanus shot after riding in this truck.

He squints at the tiny print.

"She's probably home," I say, as much to myself as Max. "The sooner I get there, the sooner she can yell 'ha ha' and you can get back to your life."

And I will get back to mine.

It's pitch-black out but you wouldn't know it from the neon Heartbreak sign, flashing on and off in the night. With each flash, I wonder where Paris has gone.

"Hey." Max peers at the scrap of paper again, still not shifting. "Oh. I get it. Clever."

"What?" I lean in. I can see the sharp creases where she'd folded the note over and over—a tiny origami triangle.

Max points to Paris's signature. "Look," he says. "The numbers."

I read them over again. 0 00 1 36. So? Max Sullivan has known my sister for like what? Thirty minutes and half a piece of pie? Not even that much since she's been missing through most of it.

Max waggles the paper as though this will help.

0 00 1 36.

"C'mon," Max says. "Think." His tone reminds me of Mr. Lippman, when he'd put a physics equation on the board.

And then I see it in my head: the wheel, red and white and black.

Of *course* I know this. My mother works in a damn casino.

0 00 1 36. The numbers on a roulette wheel.

"It can't be," I say. But I know it is.

"Your sister plays roulette?" He scowls when I snort.

"Um, no. But our mom deals blackjack. At Vegas Mike's." I frown. "Even if that's it, what would she be trying to tell me? To place a bet?"

"Well," Max begins, and I cut him off with a wave of my hand. This is not physics class. Max is cute, but I have to find my sister.

"You know what?" I say, and I know he hears the prissy in my voice. "There *is* no explanation. She's not hurt. She's not

42

missing. She's just being—well, I don't know what she's being. But I bet she's being it at home." The words fly out, but I don't know if I mean them. What if something has really happened?

"Maybe," Max says. "But aren't you at least curious?"

What is it with this boy?

"Max. You seem like a nice guy. But I don't know you. You don't know me. It's three in the morning. The last thing I want to do right now is explain my sister."

I snag the note from him, my hand bumping the Atomic Testing Museum name tag slung over the mirror. It swings back and forth between us on its twisty blue lanyard.

I edge toward the door again, hands pressed to bare knees, legs pale against the dark seat. "Why are you helping me, anyway?"

Max looks startled, brows rising over those gray eyes. But his answer comes quickly.

"You're the first girl who's ever offered me coconut cream pie," he says. "It's not the kind of thing a guy takes lightly."

I know I'm blushing and that makes me blush even more, the burn shooting to the tops of my ears. But if I'm going to believe a lie it might as well be one like this.

I tell him our address.

The Mazda is nowhere in sight when we pull up to our house—paint peeling, lawn brown and scraggly. Mom's car is still gone, too, which makes sense, but so is Tommy's Tahoe. Was it even in the driveway? Sometimes he wedges it into our crap-filled garage. It's been such a crazy night, I don't remember.

"We can drive around to casinos if you want," Max says, and I realize he's watching me. "I'll wait for you."

"And do what? Look at every roulette wheel in Vegas?"

Max purses his lips. "Maybe," he says slowly. "That's the thing about mysteries, right? You don't know until you start solving them."

"My sister is unsolvable," I tell him. He nods, but doesn't respond.

We eyeball each other. He is still cute. The sexy, mysterious scar over his eyebrow in particular. But I tell him, "Thanks for the ride," and shove open the passenger door. Our house looks empty—the windows like blank faces.

Somewhere beyond the house, the sound of a train whistle ropes long and low through the air. My chest tightens.

I hesitate, half in and half out of the truck. This whole thing . . . But still I don't walk toward the house.

"I'll go in with you," Max says. The offer hangs in the air with the train whistle.

I don't know why I consider it. But I do.

"If you want," I say, not looking at him.

We sit in silence for a few beats, desert heat pressing like a hand, the last of the train whistle barely audible.

Not until he locks the truck and follows me inside do I realize that I've been holding my breath.

SIX

TOMMY'S GLASS, A SWIRL OF AMBER-COLORED BOOZE AT THE BOTTOM, is sitting on the kitchen table as we walk in, but the house is quiet, cat clock ticking and the broken icemaker in the fridge making a useless groan.

"I'm back," I call. No one answers. I say it again, louder, just in case. Sometimes Mom gets off early if it's slow at Vegas Mike's. But it's just me and Max.

My stomach clenches. I think of telling him to leave—that I'll deal with this—but I don't.

No other note from Paris anywhere I can see, just a deck of playing cards stacked cockeyed on the table near Tommy's glass.

I catch Max's gaze flick from the cat clock to Tommy's glass to the cards. My face heats again as I wonder what he's thinking. That we're boozy cat-clock lovers who gamble and tell the occasional physics joke? Of course that last part is just me.

"My stepfather plays poker," I blurt even though Max hasn't asked.

Max says nothing, just nods. The clock, a little slow, hits three and the cat meows, making us both jump.

Max laughs. I try to and fail. Then he announces: "I play poker."

"Like tournaments?" I ask, unimpressed. "But you're not old enough." You have to be twenty-one to sit in the casinos and gamble. Everyone knows that.

He grins sweetly, fishing for his wallet. "Fake ID," he says, showing me two different pieces of plastic.

Maxwell Sullivan of Bozeman, MT, is twenty-five.

Maxwell Sullivan of Houston, TX, is eighteen.

Max leans against our grimy kitchen counter. I study the IDs. "Pretty authentic, right? That's what you're thinking."

Actually I'm thinking no way would anyone believe he's twenty-five, but people fall for all sorts of scams, even here where they should know better.

"It's just local tourneys," he says, scraping a hand through his hair. "Small-time stuff. I know better than to try the Strip casinos."

"Do you win?"

He shrugs in that way that guys who win do.

"Some. I've got a good memory. That's all. You know

Einstein played craps," he adds as though this clarifies things.

"Well," I say slowly, dragging the word out a few beats. "I guess you're lucky then."

I say the last part nicely, because I appreciate the Einstein reference as much as any other girl on the Academic Bowl team, but something sad shifts into his gray eyes.

"Poker's not about luck. It's about convincing the other guy that you're lucky. Not the same thing at all."

He follows me to Paris's room, across from mine on one side of the house, our shared bathroom at the front of the hallway that spokes down to our rooms. My heart thuds a little even though I know no one's home. Mom and Tommy's room is on the other side, the kitchen and living/dining rooms in between. Far enough from them for some privacy.

We are four people in this house: Tommy Davis, my mother, Paris, and me—"Tommy and his three girls" my mother calls it, which makes Tommy chuckle.

Max stands awkwardly at the door, tapping his thumb on the frame, then finally enters.

I poke my head in Paris's closet. I peer under her bed. Nothing seems out of place. But it's hard to tell. Dishes of beads sit on her bed, on the floor. On the small desk under the window, a hot glue gun rests on top of *British Lit Survey*, the senior English textbook Paris never returned.

On the windowsill, more necklaces: Tiny red beads

strung on black thread. Bright-red stones glued to an oblong piece of metal hanging from a thin chain. And the bin of bracelets like the one she was wearing tonight: piles of leather strands studded with sparkle. She's been working a lot these past weeks.

My foot bumps something and I half stumble, stubbing my toe on what turns out to be one of her fake snakeskin stilettos, the sharp-edged heel pointing up toward the ceiling. Her black ankle boots with the cracked soles sit neatly together smack in the middle of the room. An ugly pair of brown platform heels rests heel to toe on the carpet near the head of her bed.

Okay then. Messy room filled with crap. But all her stuff—it looks like it's still here. So she's not gone then. Just temporarily misplaced.

But the room feels chaotic, which is not like Paris. Messy, yes. Random, not really. Weird.

"She made all this?" Max scoops up a red-bead necklace, turning it over in his hand.

I nod, thinking that I'm not sure how I feel about him touching her stuff.

"She's good," he says, winding the delicate chain around two fingers. "I had no idea."

"How would you?"

Something I can't identify shifts across his face like a wisp of cloud. He sets the necklace back with the others. "What I mean is, your sister's really talented. This stuff's amazing."

"She's not named after France, you know," I say, and then regret it.

I have no idea why our mother named Paris what she did. Callie Hollings is big on impulse, short on long-term planning. I don't know what she was thinking or if she was thinking anything at all. I've never met my father, but Paris has met hers. He took her to the circus once when I was five. She came home with a stuffed elephant with a Ringling Bros. headdress and a bellyache from cotton candy.

I cried because he didn't take me, too.

But, I inform Max, the story Paris often tells is this: *Paris, Texas* was Kurt Cobain's favorite movie. "Not that she's a Cobain fan," I say. "But people always ask about her name and she'd read that once so it's her story."

"What's that movie?" Max asks. "You know, the one with 'We'll always have Paris'?"

I roll my eyes. But I liked that he said it.

"It's got a fake Eiffel Tower," I say. "Paris, Texas, I mean. My sister looked it up." Of course Vegas has a fake one, too. But Vegas has a fake everything.

"You ever been?" Max asks.

"Which one?"

He grins. "Either."

I shake my head. "You?"

"Nope, not even the Texas one, and I lived there. No Eiffel Towers in Houston. Not that I know of."

This time I feel the blush start from the hollow of my throat. Here I'm babbling about Texas and he's from there.

I turn off Paris's lamp. Max follows me into the hallway.

The door to my room is closed and I know no one's in there, but my heart stutters as I turn the knob anyway.

"Oh," Max says, peering over my shoulder because he's tall enough to do that. "You're one of those."

I swivel and look at him, both of us framed in the doorway.

"You know," he says, waggling his dark brows. "Not messy."

"Hey," I say, but he's looking beyond me to my posters, pausing to bark a laugh at *There Are Only Ten Kinds of People: Those Who Understand Binary*.

I follow his gaze—glad now that I made my bed before we left—and see him pause at the collage hanging over my headboard, a black-and-white landscape that Paris made me. The one with a woman in one of those veil things that show only her eyes.

Then he's walking to my bookshelf where he picks up the small plastic skeleton that I bought at a flea market when I was ten. I cringe because it's positioned between my Harry Potters and my old E. Nesbit paperbacks. Ones like *Half Magic*, which Paris and I loved because the kids find a magic coin and go on adventures. Books are private things until you get to know someone. But he's focused on the skeleton.

Max runs a finger over its bare ribs. "Cool."

"Don't hurt Tiny Tim," I warn him, resisting the urge

to snatch it away from him.

"Tiny Tim? You named a skeleton Tiny Tim?"

It is the name on the box he came in, but I am not about to admit that.

"I've known you for an hour," I say instead. "I think it's a little too early for snap judgments."

Of course I make judgments all the time. It's when I forget to make them that I get in trouble. But sometimes I get tired of watching and paying attention. Sometimes I want to be the girl who people do things for, even when she doesn't ask. There are girls like that, and I envy them.

"What did you do?" Max says. "Get mad at him?" He's pointing to Tiny Tim's left wrist, where I had to glue the ulna back in place. I guess I wasn't careful enough because it's just the slightest fraction off from where it should be.

"Bumped him with my elbow," I say quickly. "You're the only one who's ever noticed." I rub my arms. My index finger drags over the tiny cut Paris got so hyper about.

Max slides his gaze to my old dollhouse, the two-story wooden one Grammy Marie made me for my eighth birthday, each room painted a different color and wired with a matching tiny colored lightbulb that actually lights up when I plug it in. Even now, at night, I imagine stories for the rooms.

Paris still fashions miniature pillows and chairs and pictures for this house, placing them inside for me to find like treasures.

I don't know what I'll do if he mocks the dollhouse, but he doesn't say anything because the beep of a car remote on our driveway makes us both jump.

Paris!

"Finally," I say, rushing from my room and up the narrow hall, Max clomping in my wake. "See, I told you she'd get tired of this whole thing."

The front door swings open.

I start talking even before Paris makes it into the tiny foyer. "You are one crazy—"

"Tommy?" says my mother's voice as she steps inside. Her tone is a combination of anger and hesitation.

My heart falls, my brain still half expecting Paris to walk in after her, but my mother is alone, smelling of beer and cigarette smoke and a faint trace of Vera Wang Princess Night, the perfume Tommy bought her for her birthday.

"He went out," I say.

She's wearing her work outfit—a low-cut red tank that reads *Vegas Mike's* across the chest, tight black jeans, and red stripper heels, which she kicks off now with a groan of pleasure, sending one of them sliding across the floor. It skids to a stop in front of Max.

In the following order, I watch my mother register: Me. Tommy's almost-empty glass. Max. The cat clock, ticking past three. Then back to me, a variety of expressions flickering over her face. Just barely, I can see the vein in the middle of her forehead beating. It pops out like that when she's tired or upset. Or both.

"It's past three in the morning, Leonora," she says. Her voice tightens as she acknowledges Max. "Who are *you*?"

"Paris is missing." I dig in my pocket for the note.

"I'm Max," Max says.

"What?" asks my mother, and I'm not sure if she's questioning Paris's disappearance or Max's existence. At Vegas Mike's she's the best blackjack dealer on the floor. Quick, funny, good with the drunks. Mean when she needs to be. Tough as nails. On the other hand, she's just worked a ten-hour shift.

"Paris, Mom. I don't know where the hell she is." I fill her in on the rest of it—leaving out the driving-around part, obviously.

"Have you been out all night?" Mom asks. From the corner of my eye I see Max press his lips together. "Thought you were cramming for that SAT retake. Scholarships don't grow on trees, Leo."

I let the last part slide. "Um, no. Not all night." Technically this is true. The sun isn't up yet. "She's playing some game, I think. Paris." I wave the note.

People don't think my mother is smart, but she is, in a street-smart way. She reads people like no one I've ever seen. One quick glance at someone who sits down at her blackjack table and she *knows*.

But when Paris broke her arm dirt-biking and got hysterical while we were camping in the desert near Ridgecrest

back in Cali, I was the one who sat with her and let her
squeeze my hand, hard, until the adults—Mom and her
friends from the Harley place—sobered up enough to
drive us to the hospital.

When I told my mother I was applying to Stanford, her
first question was "What will it cost?"

Now, barely listening, she interrupts me with "Where's
Tommy?"

I shrug.

"Does he know you girls went out?"

"Yeah," I say, surprising myself. "He does."

Mom considers this briefly, pushes a strand of hair from
her forehead. "God," she says. "I need some wine." She
steps to the fridge, extracting a half-filled bottle of white
wine and pouring some into a juice glass. Our wineglasses
are all sitting dirty in the sink. She takes a long swallow.
Then another.

"You brought home a boy in the middle of the night,"
she says once she's drained the faded floral glass. Her eyes
drift back to Max, heavy lidded, roving.

"I'm helping Leo." Max steps over Mom's red platform
and moves next to me. Somehow he looks even taller in our
cramped kitchen. I realize I'm staring and look away.

Yawning now, Mom rubs a knuckle over her cheekbone—
defined and high like my sister's. Mascara is sprinkled like
dots of mud on the puffy pockets under her eyes.

"Leo," she says, looking at me sharper now, more

careful. My heart thumps against my ribs. The cat clock ticks in the background. Max clears his throat. It is one of those moments when you think that something huge is about to happen.

We are like one of those still life paintings, I think absurdly. Mother. Daughter. Strange boy. Glass of wine. A million unsaid things.

"Mom," I say, then stop.

My mother pours the rest of the wine into her glass.

"It's fine, Leo. You know your sister."

That's it? "Mom. Paris is *missing*. As in *gone*. Has she called you? She has the car. And my phone and stuff. And this weird note . . ."

I push the note at her and she scans it quickly, possibly reading, possibly just looking, while I tap my foot on the floor.

"See the roulette numbers," I say, pointing. I wait for her to say something. Do something.

Mom gestures wide with her arms—a sudden, frenetic gesture that startles me, making my heart bump harder. A few drops of wine fling into the air. "Your sister is dramatic, Leonora. She's always been dramatic." Her gaze flits back to Max. She presses two fingers to her lips, like she's holding a cigarette.

"Figure it out, Leo. Please." It's what she expects of me. "Tommy didn't say where he was going?"

I tell her no. She asks if I'm sure. I don't answer.

"Don't bring boys home if no one's here," she says then, like this is something I do all the time. The tips of my ears heat because Max is standing right here. Mom digs in her purse and pulls out her phone, thumbs flicking as she texts something. She stares at the phone, obviously waiting. When nothing happens, she dumps purse and phone on the counter, then rolls her neck until the vertebrae crack audibly.

"It'll be fine, Leo." She leaves the stripper heels and takes the wine, disappearing through the family room toward her bedroom.

The cat clock meows. Three thirty.

Max pushes at the sleeves of his blue button-down.

"Sorry," I say, not really sure what exactly I'm sorry for.

"So," Max says after a few awkward beats. He purses his lips then un-purses them. There's a tiny freckle on his forehead not far from that eyebrow scar. Like a little satellite to the half-moon. "Why would your sister make a roulette reference?"

My brain scrambles, trying to focus. He's legitimately helping me. At least he seems to want to. This does not happen in my world. Ever.

I toss the empty wine bottle in the trash under the sink, where it lands with a thud. "She wouldn't. She doesn't gamble."

"Leo." Max leans toward me, gaze solid on mine. I focus on the scar, the freckle, his eyes. My insides feel hollow and restless. I do not know what to do with a nice boy.

For a crazy second I think he's going to kiss me, and my heart sprints into my throat because for an even crazier second I think I'm going to let him. My armpits go damp, then my palms. I start to step back. Then the water pipes clank—hard—and I hear the shower in my mother's bathroom, and the moment evaporates and my brain reminds me about how nothing in this house ever feels private enough.

Like the other day when Paris thought it was Tommy in the hall bathroom even though it was only me. My sister banged on the door. "Get the hell out. I gotta pee."

I'd been shaving my legs at the sink. She knocked so hard I dropped the razor. I peeked my head out.

Paris stormed in and flopped on the toilet. My sister had no issues about stuff like that.

My towel, wrapped around me, slipped as I went back to shaving.

Paris stopped and gave me a curious look.

"What?"

"You're wearing your underwear with a towel," she said.

I rewrapped the towel around me, tighter. "Don't forget to flush," I said.

"You still want me to help you find her?" Max asks, bringing me back. "'Cause I'm in if you do." His gray eyes hold my gaze, and even though it's been a crazy night, I find myself smiling.

Maybe there really are nice boys. Maybe Max Sullivan

is one of them. That's possible, right?

But my stomach seizes anyway. What if this really is my sister's elaborate game to avoid saying good-bye? What will I do then? I tell myself not to worry. The thought feels like a lie.

Everything seems strange and right and wrong all at once. Like the world is on the edge and I'm on the edge with it, toes slipping over the line.

So I make my choice.

"I guess," I say. "Yeah. If that's okay?"

A smile tilts his lips a little, and then full-out. "You and me, Leo, we're a team. Like carbon and hydrogen."

I stare at him like he's crazy, which possibly he is.

Or maybe I am, to trust him.

"We're bonded," he finishes.

SEVEN

IN THE RANGER AGAIN, MAX CRANKS THE ENGINE, KEYS JANGLING, AND asks where Paris and I go when we drive around. Maybe we should start there, he says, and I list them for him: Fremont Street. The Strip. The all-night coffee place. Devil Doughnuts that opens at 4:00 a.m. But which one?

"Just drive," I say. "Let me think." I tap my fingers on the door handle, trying to give my adrenaline somewhere to go, then clutch my hands together to stop them from shaking.

Max arches that scarred brow, then adjusts the rearview mirror—which ends up still cockeyed—and we back out of our driveway and head down the block. He snaps on the radio, roaming until he finds some old Keith Urban song.

I flash him a look, but he grins that grin and says, "He's a genius on the guitar. Also I'm from Texas. Country music is a requirement."

"Like they test you? Or deport you for hip-hop?" I say, trying for clever and ending this side of geeky.

"Yup." He drawls the word, and for the first time I hear just a hint of southern in his voice.

"You guys all drive trucks, too, right?"

"That would be *y'all*. And yes. But only when we're not riding our horses."

This time I'm the one grinning. Something like butterflies tickles inside my chest.

"You from here?"

I shake my head. "California."

Another smile. "Surfer girl, right?"

I roll my eyes.

Max hands me his phone. "Try your sister again."

I call Paris's number. This time her voice mail picks up on the first ring. "This is Paris. You know what to do."

It's just a recording, but my pulse leaps at the sound of her voice.

"Call me back at this number, damn it," I say. "Paris. Enough. It's not funny."

On the radio, Keith Urban shifts into Kacey Musgraves, who tells me to "follow your arrow." This feels overly optimistic right now. Paris likes that song of hers about the waitress blowing smoke.

"Was your sister unhappy?" Max asks out of the blue, eyes on the road.

I glance at him sharply. "No. Why?"

"Was she happy?" His voice sounds serious and curious and something else I can't quite name. If he's trying to figure her out, he'll be working the problem for a long time.

"No." I unclasp my hands to rub the back of my neck, fingers tracing the spiky edges of my hair. "She was in that middle place. Not unhappy. Not happy. You know."

He nods. "Yeah," he says. "I do." He doesn't elaborate.

"I have to work at eleven," I say, because if he's a rational human being, any second now he's going to say, *Hey, Leo. This has been fun and all, but your sister is your business and I'll see you around. Come on by the museum, maybe.*

I watch his hands on the wheel, thumbs splayed, and realize that I'm wondering what they would feel like against my cheek.

For the next few blocks, I remind myself that Max Sullivan has a limited shelf life.

I wish I didn't like looking at the tiny scar above his left eyebrow. I wish I'd never brought him the coconut cream pie. Him helping me is complicating things and things are already complicated enough.

We reach the edge of our neighborhood, stopping with a quick jolt at the intersection. I need to make up my mind about where we're going.

"I have to ask," Max says, voice serious again.

"What?" I look at him. His face looks serious, too.

"Are you team zombie or team ninja?" He points at my shirt.

A beat passes as I flush red to the tips of my ears.

Nothing like a T-shirt that proclaims my absolute nerdom.

"Ninjas," I say, trying and failing to sound cleverly ironic. "It's the stealth factor. Plus they eat pie."

But Max laughs—this happy burst of sound that ricochets around the truck. So happy that I start giggling, just a little, and then we're both cracking up the way people do at four in the morning over stupid stuff.

Only we're still sitting at the stop sign.

"Well," he says after a bit. "Where to?"

I shrug, then slip Paris's note from my pocket. She can't seriously think I'm going to go visit every casino in Vegas looking at their roulette wheels. There has to be something else.

I go over the words sentence by sentence, like I do with a math problem. What does it say? What does it mean?

Stay calm, Leo. Well, that's clear. But the *"he's making me"* part? Is that real? Or just Paris bullshit? My sister doesn't let boys, or anyone, tell her what to do. Is "this"—whatever this is—the "only way"? I don't know. Maybe it's a game? My sister making the boring, ordinary world more palatable.

Max watches me, waiting.

"I don't know," I tell him, because clearly he expects me to tell him something. "Shit. Maybe you should just take me home. This is ridiculous. I . . ."

My gaze drops to the note again.

And then the whole thing makes sense in the sudden way things do when I'm trying to remember something for a test and I know I've seen it or heard it but it's dangling just out of reach. Until it isn't.

"There!" I jab my finger against my sister's signature. "Look!" *xParis 0 00 1 36.* Of course. How did I not see it?

"Slow down there, Sparky," he says, southern boy drawling. "You figure it out?"

"I'm an idiot," I announce cheerfully. I feel buoyant, a helium balloon set free. "It's been there all along. I just didn't—it's her name and the roulette numbers."

"Well, yeah." He wrinkles his forehead.

"Max!" He is seriously the worst detective ever. "She's not just signing her name, see. She's telling us where the roulette wheel is."

His forehead is still pinched, the tiny scar scrunching in this way that I totally shouldn't care about right now. And then his eyes go wide and bright.

"Paris?"

"Exactly. I hope, anyway." I feel a brief twinge of nerves.

"Only one way to find out."

My heart is hopping. Is she going to bet money so she can leave? Con someone over twenty-one to put it all on red for her, spin the wheel, hoping for the best?

That would be Paris. Not crazy enough for an inside bet, but believing in the odds anyway.

Is that the plan? Does it include coming back for me?

Max punches the gas, and we fly through the intersection, the Ranger bouncing hard, hang a right, and head to the Strip for the second time tonight.

"Paris Hotel, mademoiselle?" Max asks in a cheesy French accent.

"*Oui*," I say, going with it.

In the truck bed, a half-squashed Big Gulp cup bounces out, escaping.

"If you help me find her," I say, "I'm going to get this truck detailed for you."

"*Ooh la la,*" says Max Sullivan.

EIGHT

THE SUN IS PUSHING AT THE HORIZON BY THE TIME WE HIT LAS VEGAS Boulevard, rising into the neon haze. But the air is cooler now, and Max has rolled down the windows. The Strip is emptying out. Even hard-core gamblers take a break at some point. A guy in a sleeveless shirt and cargo shorts weaves along the sidewalk clutching a tall glass of what looks like strawberry daiquiri. A thick-sized middle-aged couple stands near the street, leaning in to each other, yelling.

"You bet it all," the woman hollers. She's wearing white capris and a shapeless light-blue T-shirt that says *I Love My Doberman*. "I can't believe that you bet everything on the goddamned craps table."

"Babe," he screams, arms out, cupping his hands like maybe he's waiting for poker chips to fall from the sky. "I felt lucky."

The air smells like desert and money. I should be tired, but I'm wide-awake.

We're going to the Paris Casino. Gotcha, Paris Hollings. This scavenger hunt is about to be over.

Classical music fills the air from the Bellagio Fountains across the street, even though the fountains aren't running. It crescendos loudly as though to punctuate capri lady's shouting. Rachmaninoff, maybe? I'm not sure. A memory surfaces briefly of my fifth-grade orchestra teacher telling us that Sibelius put Finland on the map. I make a mental note to review composers when this is all over.

We park the truck and hike to the front of the hotel. It's a long walk. Everything in Vegas is like that—this illusion of intimacy when really it's distant and far away. I use Max's phone again and try Paris's cell. Still voice mail. I call my mother, who also doesn't answer, but I leave a message, telling her to call this number if Paris comes home.

It's well after four now and in less than seven hours I have to be at Yogiberry for another eight-hour shift, wearing a stupid black-and-pink-striped shirt and recommending the mochi topping because Kyle the manager needs us to get rid of it before it goes stale. It's a hard sell. Mochi tastes like pencil eraser. Only chewier.

But the more I work, the more money I make. The more money I make, the more I'll have for a contingency plan if Stanford doesn't give me as much aid as I hope. So I need to be there. And this makes my stomach twist. Because what if it's time to go to work and we still haven't found her?

As if he read my mind, Max says, "I'm scheduled to do two private tours today, starting at noon. There's a day camp coming to the museum and then some physics summer school class."

I scrunch my nose. "You show the Bikini Atoll exploding to impressionable little day campers?"

He looks at me deadpan. "You betcha. Blows 'em out of their seats. Literally. I always get there early to crank up the air machine for the big groups."

"You ever think that maybe you shouldn't be so happy about that?"

"Excuse me for loving my job."

He has me there. I am not in love with the frozen yogurt industry.

Or with tourists who drop stuff on the sidewalk, like the crumpled Fatburger bag I half trip over now because I'm looking up at the hotel.

"Careful," Max says, and his hand goes to the small of my back.

"Don't," I say, stepping out of reach. "I'm fine."

He shoots me a glance.

The Paris Hotel and Casino looms in front of us, its fifty-story replica of the Eiffel Tower lifting into the night sky. Some of the legs actually poke through the roof into the casino. A huge hot-air balloon, hovering over a fake version of the Arc de Triomphe, serves as a light-up marquee.

At the Arc Bar, you can buy a souvenir beverage in a plastic glass shaped like the Eiffel Tower. And there's this touristy restaurant where Tommy took us to lunch the first day we moved here. He and Mom shared a ridiculously large plum-colored drink called Purple Passion that they slurped with straws. After that, we all went shopping at the Miracle Mile, and then to the movies, where Tommy bought us the extra-large tub of popcorn—the one we never got because it cost too much. "He's nice," I whispered to Mom, my mouth full of greasy popcorn.

A sign announces that you can pay to ride to the top of the tower—*Most Romantic View of Las Vegas*, it says—although I've never done it. Tourists do all sorts of things that people who live in places never do. Like I bet people born in New York City live their whole lives and never go to the top of the Empire State Building.

Of course, at this hour, the top is closed. And even if it were open, I'd still have a problem, not that I tell this to Max. But the truth is, I'm afraid of heights. It's not like I'm *totally* phobic. Just that my heart rate is more normal when my feet are on the ground and I don't think I'm going to vom or faint because my head feels all light and fuzzy.

The red awning over the front door reads *Le Casino*, which only someone from Iowa or North Dakota who hasn't gotten out much would think is authentic to France.

"Let's go," I say, feeling antsy. The sooner we're in, the sooner we find my sister.

I half expect to see her as we walk in the door. But we don't. Not even when we race over to the roulette wheel— empty except for the dealer. My stomach sinks so quick it surprises me.

"Scavenger hunt!" Max says, suddenly too loud and enthusiastic, like maybe this is all getting old. My stomach dips again. I pretend it didn't.

We backtrack. We poke around the huge fake French lobby, our feet sliding on slick marble tile.

My sister is not in Le Reception. She is not in front of Le Central Lobby Bar. She is not at Le Theater or Les Toilettes. She is not lined up on the fake French cobblestones under the fake French streetlamp waiting to beat the breakfast rush at Le Buffet, observing the fake night sky that's painted on the fake French ceiling.

"Where the fuck are you?" I mean to keep this in my head, not shout it out, but that's exactly what I do.

One of the guys at Le Reception leans over the counter and asks if we need something.

"Looking for my sister," I say, trying to keeping my voice even while my pulse zips race-car fast. I describe her to him.

"What's her name?" he asks. Actually, what he says is "What *eez* her name, mademoiselle?" which I think *eez* taking *zee* whole thing too far.

"Paris," I say, and he gives a fake French body shrug— probably because I'm looking for a girl named Paris at the

Paris Hotel—and helpfully informs us that the Eiffel Tower will be open after nine.

My pulse zooms faster. Maybe I was wrong about the roulette wheel and the signature. I'm about to give up when Max—who's been looking at his phone and not even paying attention to me or the concierge—says, "Let's walk the casino again," and I agree even though this makes me edgy. Paris and I have done our share of underage casino wandering these past few months, but it never pays to push things.

I know they watch from cameras in the ceiling—even at Vegas Mike's security is pretty stiff, although nothing like the big hotels, at least according to Mom, who last week had to Taser some huge drugged-up guy who kept grabbing this woman's boobs at Mom's blackjack table. The lone security guard on duty held him down and tossed Mom the Taser, hollering, "Just press the damn thing, Callie. Now." Which somehow I doubt is actual casino safety policy.

I start another round of the casino, racewalking now, almost running.

"Slow down, Leo," Max says. "Wouldn't want to lose you, too." This seems an odd thing to say, but it's been an odd night.

"Look for notes," I tell him as we wander past a trio of old ladies with fanny packs and home-permed gray hair all playing one of those loud multiline slots that whoosh out 3-D images of animals when you hit it big. I'm trying to think like my sister, which is not easy since we do not think at all alike. "And silver Sharpie," I shout over the din. "Or Hello Kitty Band-Aids."

"Okay," Max says, but he pauses at a Double Diamond machine and, taking his time about it, methodically drops in three quarters. One. Two. Three. My shoulders tense. I don't have time for this.

I hover at his elbow, tapping my foot on the carpet, while he glances away from the machine, looking around leisurely like he's a tourist with no particular agenda. Then he presses Play 3. He hasn't even sat down on the stool.

Should I say something? He's the one driving.

The bar rolls. One double diamond. Two double diamonds. Three double diamonds. *Click. Click. Click.*

The slot machine starts ringing like a fire engine.

Max has hit le jackpot.

Ring! Ding! Ring! Clang!

Seriously?

One hundred. Two hundred. Three hundred.

Money. So much money!

"Max!" He's gawking at the machine, but when I say his name, he grabs my hand and squeezes, then lets go and jumps up and down like he's on one of those game shows. I try to look happy for him and fail.

The machine keeps dinging. The dollars keep rolling.

"Yes!" Max shouts over the clanging, pumping his fist in the air. "I can't believe this!"

A tired-looking cocktail waitress saunters over. She looks Max up and down, studying him for a few long beats. "Show me your ID," she says, not in a French accent.

"I'm not ordering a drink," Max tells her. The Double Diamond machine continues to clang like an out-of-control fire engine. Max stands up straighter, but she's wearing four-inch heels, so they're still eye to eye.

"ID," Cocktail Waitress says again, louder this time.

Max digs his wallet from his pocket. Fishes out his ID. Double Diamond clangs and bangs.

I stare at the flashing numbers on the top of the slot machine. Fifteen hundred dollars.

Fifteen hundred dollars! Not as much as I have saved in my secret closet hiding spot, but still. Not bad.

In the perfect world, the tired-looking cocktail waitress would look at Max's fake ID and accept without further argument that he was indeed twenty-something Max from Bozeman, Montana. She would hand Max the pay-out ticket. Paris would appear in the lobby, having tired of secretly riding the monorail back and forth to the MGM, and we would all laugh at the funny evening we'd been having. And Max would cut me in for half since he wouldn't have been there had it not been for me.

Instead, security appears.

"You're underage, sir," says the tallest of the beefy security guards, the one with an unattractive comb-over. "You need to leave. If you don't leave, we will call the cops."

"Aw, c'mon," Max says.

"Get the hell out, sir." Comb-Over Guy's eyes go squinty, like he's only just realized I'm standing there, clearly even more underage than the boy with the fake ID—which he promptly confiscates.

"We're looking for my sister," I tell him primly.

Comb-Over peers down his nose at me. "By playing slots?"

He has a point.

We are escorted through Le Lobby, past Le Reception, out to Le Exit, and instructed that if we choose to pull this again, we will be permanently banned for life from Paris.

"The hotel?" I ask, not under my breath.

And then we're out on the street, and we're both laughing because there is something perfect about being banned for life from Paris, which at this moment is absolutely fine with me.

Max shoves a hand through his already messy dark hair. "Sorry," he says, but his eyes are still bright from the jackpot.

I know I should thank him for at least trying. For taking me here and at least pretending to care. But it all seems a waste now and I bite back the annoyance that's rising.

I don't always take my mother's advice these days, but one thing she says cannot be denied: if it looks too good to be true, it probably is.

Cute boys do not drop from the sky into the Heartbreak Hotel Diner precisely when you need them to solve the mystery of your crazy sister.

"We have to go back inside," I say, knowing we can't, and suddenly it's not funny anymore. "Shit."

"Leo," Max says gently. "She's not in there. It's okay. You'll figure it out."

But he says "you" and not "we" and somehow this disappoints me even though, what did I expect?

I turn to go back to the truck, but Max's warm hand rests on my shoulder. "Slow down, Leo," he says, using my name that way for the second time tonight. "Don't worry." Hand still on my shoulder—which I'm not sure I like but don't brush away—he nudges me to the left. "Over here," he says. "I just want to stop and savor the moment, okay? You don't win a jackpot you can't keep every night, you know."

I want to keep moving, but he sounds so sincere that I follow him to the outside leg of the fake Eiffel Tower— right past the entrance to Eiffel Tower Wine and Spirits. He leans against the low cement wall and so do I, feeling suddenly like I might cry, which I am not doing.

When a minute passes and then another and Max is still basking in his non-win, I slide down and flop to the sidewalk. Might as well sit until he realizes that this is a lost cause.

I'm surprised when he folds his long legs to sit next to me. He looks oddly relaxed, casual even, like we do this all the time.

It's almost morning.

Paris is still missing.

Max cuts his eyes to me. I look away. This has been a bad idea all around.

But right now it is still preferable to going home.

And then Max shouts, "Hey!" leaning across me, his face very close.

"Look," he says, his warm breath tickling my skin. I smell lemons still. And cotton. And boy. He leans almost against my shoulder, pointing to the right.

Even though I tell it not to, my heart is pounding from his nearness.

"Get up," Max says, pulling at my arm. His voice is kind, but I yelp, "Don't," and shove him away. He drops my arm like it's on fire.

"I just . . . Sorry." He blushes in a way that makes me think that maybe he is. He points over my shoulder again. "Look," he repeats as I swivel, and he pats his hand on the cement under the Eiffel Tower leg.

My breath quickens.

Silver marker.

Silver marker!

"Does your sister have a thing for legs?" Max quips, but I ignore him, reading the tiny, precise silver Sharpie print-ing that can only be my sister's.

My heart drums against my rib cage.

You made it, she's written.

And a Hello Kitty Band-Aid—how did I not notice it?—taped over another intricately folded piece of paper.

I pull the note free and carefully unfold it, my pulse like rocket fuel in my veins.

> You're a Big Shot, little sister. You have
> to be if you've made it this far. Keep
> going, Leo. Find me. Hurry.
> xoxoParis

My heart pounds so hard my ribs hurt. It's Paris's handwriting. I'm positive. She's got to be close. Like somehow watching me, maybe.

I think I should be furious, but instead something loosens in my chest. It's just a goofy joke then. She's not actually in trouble.

I dash to the curb, Max following, his boots tapping hard on the pavement. At Las Vegas Boulevard, I squint in the hazy dawn light for our Mazda, half expecting Paris to drive by the Bellagio, waving at us and laughing.

But she doesn't. When did she put this here? Wouldn't someone else have seen it by now or bumped it or moved it or whatever? Everything inside me feels jittery and dislodged, like waves rolling. Is this still a game? If not, then what?

"Big Shot?" Max says now, snapping me back to him and the note and the ever-growing mystery that is my sister. "Does she call you Big Shot?"

"No," I tell him.

"You gotta go on it," says a woman's voice from a few feet away.

Max and I turn, the note still in both our hands, tethering us together.

It's the lady in the white capris and the Doberman T-shirt. She's practically next to us, standing not far from the *Most Romantic View of Las Vegas* sign. Has she been out here the whole time? Is that possible? Where's the guy she was yelling at?

"You're talking about the ride, right?" she says, strolling over like we're the best of friends. "The Big Shot. Shoots you up over Vegas. I'd do it again, but my Murray just bankrupted us at the craps table."

"Big Shot?" I take the note from Max and feel better when it's in my hands.

"Top of the Stratosphere," says Doberman lady. "Scares the shit out of you. But in a good way, you know?"

"Leo," Max says, eyes on me.

"I know," I tell him, and this time I smile before he does.

"Big Shot," we say in unison. I wave the note in his face.

"You're a genius," Max tells Doberman lady.

Then we're sprinting toward the truck, Max and me. I look back, briefly, at the cement block with my sister's writing on it. There is something unsettling in leaving it there—like a private part of us lying naked to the world.

The sky's getting lighter and the neon lights are fading, and I'm so tired that I'm not tired anymore.

We pound the pavement to the parking lot.

"You still want to do this?" I ask, even though I realize with a rush so strong it feels like a desert windstorm that I don't want him to say no.

"All in," Max says.

We're at the truck now. I look at him. He looks at me. Somewhere deep inside me, a small voice says I need to be careful.

But being careful doesn't always work out, does it?

"It's got to be where she is," I say, climbing into the passenger seat. I say it like I'm certain.

"Agreed." Max throws the truck in gear and we lurch into the dawn.

NINE

THE STRATOSPHERE HOTEL SITS ON THE NORTH END OF LAS VEGAS Boulevard, nearer to downtown, which my mother calls the dirty heart of Vegas. She says that it's the glitter without the pretty, but if I ever wanted to win big on penny slots, that's where I should go. My mother imparts advice like this, often deeper than she seems capable of.

Still, she's right: the closer to downtown you drive, the more low-rent Vegas becomes. Places that sell six-pound burritos and the World's Largest Gift Shop and a bunch of squat, ugly little motels.

I don't know how tall the Stratosphere is, but one way or another the rides all dangle over Vegas for some long terrifying seconds.

I should tell Max about my fear of heights.

But even as I'm working myself up to it, he announces,

"I've got an idea," and starts punching numbers into his phone. "You need to trust me, okay?"

My stomach knots at that last part but Max's gaze fixes on mine in this way that makes me nod and tell him, "Okay." His dark hair is spiking randomly and the tender skin under his eyes looks bruised. I find myself wondering if Max, like me, has stayed up all night a lot lately.

"It's Max," Max says to whoever he's called.

He's practically shouting because the Stratosphere, even at this hour, is crazy noisy—louder than the Paris. Slot machines everywhere. Blue neon-lettered signs at ceiling height directing you up this ramp or down that one or up an escalator or toward the elevators.

"No. Not tonight," Max bellows into the cell. "Tomorrow, maybe. Out in Henderson. Yeah, that same place. But hey, I need a favor, okay? It's gonna sound kind of strange."

I have no idea who he's talking to, but I listen as he says he's with this girl and he really needs to take her up to the top of the Stratosphere and maybe get her on one of those rides, like the Big Shot, and if he could do it before the sun comes up well—and here he lowers his voice and gives an annoying chuckle—he's pretty sure he can get her to put out before he has to buy her breakfast.

Something inside me freezes, and I step back into the crowd, but Max reaches for me with his free hand and wiggle-waggles his eyebrows in some kind of message that hopefully is saying, "This is just bullshit, Leo. Don't run."

"You know women," Max says into the phone. "Get them scared and let them hold on to you and before you know it . . ." He chuckles again, and the tone of his voice makes me want to kick him where it counts even though his crazy eyebrow routine has mostly convinced me he's making this up so whoever he's talking to—someone connected to an elevator key?—will help us get to the Big Shot without having to wait five hours.

"You will? Awesome, dude. We'll head right over there. I owe you. Yeah, I know. Yeah, sure. Absolutely, buddy."

He presses end and shoves the phone into his pocket. Does a stompy happy dance. Including an awkward but somehow still cute twirl. "Damn," he says. "I'm good."

I narrow my eyes. "At what? Sounding like a jerk?"

Max grins apologetically. "Sorry about that. You have to know Nate. Not that I really do, but—I play poker with him. He waits tables at the Top of the World, but he's dead broke right now after last week's poker game, so I know he's picking up some extra shifts at the twenty-four-hour diner." He gestures in what I assume is the general direction of the diner.

A thought occurs. "You won the poker game."

Max's cheeks redden, two blotchy circles. "Yeah. I did."

"He just asked you for money, didn't he?" Before we lived with Tommy Davis, I might not have put this particular two and two together. But now it seems obvious.

"Not much," he says, but he scratches the back of his head, clearly faking casual.

"Not much is still something. And it's still your money. Not mine."

We stare at each other as a small but steady stream of early-morning tourists shuffle around us.

"Nate's meeting us by the gift shop," Max says. He rattles off more information: Nate the poker-playing waiter is one of those guys who always knows how to bend the rules, find the key, whatever. He's going to take us to the top.

"'Cause you're paying him."

"It's no big deal, Leo. Just twenty bucks."

"Only twenty? I'll pay you back," I insist. What's another twenty dollars, right? I think of Tommy's fifty, lost into the night. No way will I let Max pay some guy on my behalf.

I wait for him to tell me to calm down or to spout one of those phrases that mean nothing like, *It's cool,* but he doesn't. In my personal experience, people who tell you to calm down generally do so to divert your attention from the fact that they've done something shitty that's causing you to be pissed off in the first place.

"Leo," Max says. "I . . ." He looks confused about something. "Maybe I—" He shakes his head. He doesn't finish his thought, says only, "Just so you know. Nate's kind of a jackass."

"There's a lot of that going around," I say.

* * *

Nate meets us at Viva Vegas Gifts. He's thin and rangy and pale, with washed-out blond hair and green eyes. He's also a little high, at least in my opinion, and smells like a combination of Cool Ranch Doritos and stale coffee.

"I shouldn't be doing this," he whispers loudly, but anyone can see he's the kind of guy that *absolutely* does things he's not supposed to. "Anything for love, right?"

I make an annoyed throat-clearing sound, but he either doesn't notice or he's not one for subtlety, because he keeps on talking.

"You meet her at a game?" he asks, leering at Max like I'm not there.

"Can you take us up there?" A muscle in Max's jaw flickers.

"You paying?"

Max hands him a twenty.

"We need to see the Big Shot," I say, and I hate that my voice comes out high-pitched. "The ride," I add idiotically. "Can we look at it?"

Nate smiles in that icky sly way that guys have when they think they're getting away with something or about to look at porn. "You can touch it, too," he says, and I feel a stab of nerves, like electrical wires coiling in my belly. Max shoots him a look.

There's more that he says, but I stop listening. Concentrate on not looking like I'm hyperventilating as we approach the elevator that will zoom us to the 108th floor. I can do this. Piece of cake. Or pie.

"You okay?" Max squeezes my hand.

"Hmm," I say, not committing.

Nate puffs out his skinny chest. "I can let you ride," he says. "Made a copy of Ricky's key."

Ricky, I assume, is in charge of something up top.

Max harrumphs. "He give you a key to the security cameras, too? Wouldn't want you to get in trouble, right?" His tone says that nothing would make him happier than getting Nate in trouble.

"Not a problem, man." Nate's skinny lips twitch and he looks left and right and finally at Max and me. He runs his fingers through his hair. "They do a few test runs early in the morning."

Another restless, twisty jolt in my gut. I have no time for idiots like Nate. I don't *trust* idiots like Nate. Does *Max*? That seems impossible, but what do I know? I think briefly of my short-lived relationship with cheap, bad-kisser Buddy Lathrop. My ability to assess guys is not exactly the stuff of legends.

"Let's go," I say, working to keep my voice even. "Unless you're bullshitting."

"She's a feisty one," Nate tells Max, winking. To me: "Nice shirt, by the way. Got that ninja and that zombie right out there, don't you?"

Which is a not-so-veiled comment about the size of my boobs.

"Shut the fuck up." I glare at Nate, who glares back, but with a look of resignation. Nate must get told to "shut the fuck up" a lot.

In the elevator, I look straight ahead, not raising my eyes to watch the floor numbers whiz by.

"Leo?" Max says, his voice a question.

"Afraid of heights," I admit, not elaborating. My ears pop and I force a few dry-mouthed swallows to un-pop them. We bounce to a stop on 108 and the doors slide open.

Max's phone buzzes and I jump because I left his number for Mom. But it's a text, and he types something, then shoves the phone into his pocket.

"It's an awesome view," Max says, hand on my back in a surprisingly gentle way. He placed it there somewhere during my ear popping. "You'll see."

I suck a tight breath through my teeth and step out behind Nate, who's leading the way. I decide to blame my fear and wooziness on Nate's general existence in the world.

The sun is up, heating the sky in a way that feels too close. My heart races and skips and races some more, but I tell myself: get over it. Your sister has the attention span of a gnat. No way will she keep going with this thing. It's almost morning. She wouldn't just leave me—especially not way up here. She's been running ahead of us, obviously, leaving clues. This is the kind of shit she loves. Life isn't exciting enough? Create one that is. But Paris and I, we look out for each other. That's what we do.

We shook on it once, when we first moved to Vegas. Paris started having these nightmares, and I'd wake up in the middle of the night and there she'd be, sitting on the edge of my bed, shivering. "What did you dream?" I'd ask her, only she would always say she didn't remember. Maybe it was the truth. I don't know.

"Tell me a story," she'd say, because I was good at that and so that's what I would do. "But it can't be about us," she'd add, so I made stuff up for her and pretended it was about other people, even though in my head, I knew it was sort of about us. Two girls who had a pet dragon. Two sisters who got lost at Disneyland. Sometimes we'd sit on the floor in front of my old dollhouse and I'd set the stories in those rooms. Always they had a happy ending. That's how Paris liked it. Eventually, she would be calmer and drift off to sleep. Usually so would I.

One night I was going to sleep at Natalie's.

"What if I have a bad dream?" Paris asked.

"Tell yourself a story," I said. "I can't always be here."

"But if I really needed you?" she persisted.

"Always," I told her. And we spit in our palms like we'd seen someone do in a movie and shook on it.

That's the way it was.

I look around again. It's too quiet. The place is empty. No Paris. Just a guy in coveralls tinkering with one of the rides.

"She's not here," I say to Max, pointedly ignoring Nate, who is watching this all unfold. He looks befuddled, and why shouldn't he? He'd expected romance, not this. "How could she not be here?"

"Maybe somewhere," Max says vaguely, looking around, and I yell, "No!" because it's obvious she's not. Max looks down at his boots.

Nate says, "Lovers' spat," in this singsong voice, and without warning, Max shoves him—a quick push of hands against chest.

"Dude," Nate says.

"Don't," I say.

"Leave her be," Max tells Nate, his voice a low and dangerous growl. A series of thoughts race through my head: Max has a temper. A quick one. Nate is an asshole. My sister is still missing.

They stare each other down while my gaze shifts to the Big Shot—a huge red-and-white tower (World's Highest Thrill Ride!) on top of the already huge Stratosphere Tower, with seats we could strap ourselves into and zoom to the top, then free-fall, which maybe if I'd had enough wine coolers or reefer might be possible if only we weren't already on the 108th floor.

And then I see it on the otherwise pristine white railing. My heart skips a beat.

There is no mistaking the tight, neatly printed writing. No mistaking the now-familiar silver Sharpie. I want to run to it, but my feet are still stuck to the ground. We are so damn high up.

Paris has been here. So why not stay? Why not end this?

"You're kidding me," says Max Sullivan, walking swiftly toward the ride. He shoves his hand through his already messy hair.

Nate has wandered off to talk to the guy in the coveralls. Has he seen my sister up here? The security cameras would show her, right? My head is spinning with it all.

I run my fingers over each silver letter. My pulse is in my ears, throbbing with my heartbeat, which is going very, very fast.

I knew you could do it, Leo.

Do what? Find the note? Walk around up here so high off the ground? What, Paris? What? I press a hand to my chest, willing my heart to slow the hell down.

My gaze lands on the other tiny folded slip of paper, affixed with yet another Hello Kitty Band-Aid.

Max unsticks it and hands it to me. Unlike my own sweaty hand, his is cool and dry as his fingers brush mine.

It's a receipt from the Heartbreak. Not ours, but some random tally of what someone else ate and paid for in cash. A double-cheeseburger basket, a Coke, a Cobb salad, and a Children's Pancake Platter, those ones where they put a face on top with chocolate chips and a cherry for the nose.

On the back, scrawled this time, but still Paris's handwriting, as though she was writing fast, with missing letters and scratch outs, is this: *Near the water, Leo. Remember? That's where we were happy, right? You and me. Sisters.*

Max squints at the note, frowning. "What does that mean?"

"I don't know."

"You *have* to know."

"Why?" I clench my hand around the note. "Are you the expert on what I should and shouldn't know about *my* sister?"

"You wanna go up?" The question is Nate's, who has returned and is now looking at us expectantly.

We both ignore him.

But what I can't ignore is this: I need to find her before I'm due at work. If I don't go to work, I won't get paid. I am officially sick and tired of this whole thing. I am tired of not sleeping. I am tired of pretending that it's perfectly normal that we drive around Vegas all night. Paris is making this scavenger hunt up as she goes along.

Near the water. We used to live near the water in Cali. No mystery there.

But the words from the first note flash: *"He's making me."* My lungs feels too small. What if this isn't just my sister being her flaky self? What if something has actually happened? What if this is all . . . real?

"I didn't write that shit over there," Nate informs the guy in the coveralls. "So don't you go blaming it on me."

I realize again how high up we are—how far it is to the ground.

"Let's go," I tell Max. "I need to get down from here." I turn back to the elevator, but suddenly everything's a blur. My heart is racing and sweat prickles cold at my hairline. The tightness has migrated to my throat. I press my hand to my chest again. There's not enough air.

You know what this is, I tell myself. *You're just afraid. Walk it off. It's just a tall building.*

"Leo?" Max sounds far away.

I bend at the waist, but it doesn't help. Every piece of me feels both jagged and numb.

And then his arms are wrapped around me.

"I've got you," Max says. "Just breathe, okay. I've got you. Don't worry, Leo. Do you hear me? Breathe."

He keeps holding tight and somehow we're on the elevator without Nate and going down, down, down so fast that my ears pop again and my fingers feel tingly and I still can't get a good breath, but Max doesn't remove his arms. "Breathe with me, Leo," he says, hugging me and my zombie-and-ninja shirt against his chest and somehow my empty lungs fills with air because I'm following the in and out of Max's oxygen. The steady sound of his heartbeat thumps against my own floundering heart.

"Shit," I say against Max's chest. "Why is she doing this?"

His arms are still around me as the doors open and we stumble out and back into the hotel, almost sideswiping a woman wearing what looks like the ugliest prom dress ever. It's floor length and purple and strapless and covered with enough sequins that it makes my eyes hurt.

"You're breathing," Max says, voice gentle. He lets me go.

Hands on hips, I inhale deeply. Then press two fingers to my stomach and inhale again, this time through my nose. Everything seems to be working. Including my utter humiliation at this happening in front of Max. The thought makes my stomach dip.

I focus on the lady in purple who sits down at a Pai Gow table, passes the dealer some money, then rests her head in her arms. Watching her both settles me and makes me sad. I know how it is to want something so fiercely it tangles your insides, making the rest of your life feel shabby and small.

"She's just messing with you, I bet," Max says, and for a second I think he means the lady in purple. But he's talking about Paris.

"I don't know. She's never—none of this is like her." The words are both a lie and the truth. It is totally like her. But not like this.

Max purses his lips. "I think you had a panic attack, Leo Leonora."

"No kidding. And it's Hollings." The words come out sounding brittle and angry. Does he think he's being cute with the two names? Maybe he is—a little.

"I'm sorry," I tell him then, because I don't know what else to say. "About the whole . . . thank you. You didn't need . . . thank you." I turn away. I don't know what to do with nice boys who hold tight when I'm freaking out and act like it's no big deal.

We're back on Las Vegas Boulevard now, the sun firmly set in the pale sky, a steady stream of people headed into the IHOP down the block. A vague scent of bacon frying wafts our way. The air is cool, but underneath, a heat presses against my skin.

"I know how it feels to be out of control," Max says, looking down and then back at me. It is the first truly personal thing he's told me. "I don't know if that's panic. But that's why you have to breathe—"

"I don't like heights."

"Okay." Max draws out the word like he's waiting for me to say more.

"It's a long story. We need to go."

But there is something about the way that thin scar sits on his eyebrow and how his hair is now curling right at his ears, and how the bright desert sunlight dances across the tiny dusting of freckles on his nicely shaped nose. He smells good still—not like anything in particular anymore, just boy. And as he rubs his neck, his long fingers brush against a strand of curl.

"I had a bad experience with a Ferris wheel," I say, and

when he doesn't fill the space of my silence after, I add: "Couple years ago. We were at the Arizona State Fair. My stepfather thought it was funny to rock the car when we were stuck on top. I'd just had this greasy funnel cake. And . . . I don't know. It felt like we were tipping, and the door wasn't on right and . . . I got scared. Stupid, right? But it stuck with me."

I sound silly and babyish, I think. Everyone rocks the car at the top, right?

Max is quiet for a moment, then says, "People do dumb shit." He keeps his eyes on me. "Was Paris scared, too?"

I get quiet, too, thinking. "No," I tell him after a few beats. Then: "Mad, actually. But she laughed . . . Whatever. I felt like a dork." I do not tell him how what I remember after that was my mother bitching because later I upchucked that funnel cake Tommy had bought me.

I attempt a jaunty tone. "But then this dude got his arm broken by his opponent at the Arm Wrestling World Championship area right next to the Spam Mobile," I say. "That pretty much distracted everybody. It was a huge cracking sound. His arm went like this." I demonstrate, and Max wrinkles his freckled nose. The sun shines on him some more.

"I'm not trying to rock the Ferris wheel," he says.

He leans close, then closer.

I wonder again about what it would be like to kiss him. Is he wondering the same thing—this boy that I've known for just a few hours? The thought edges sharply at me, both hopeful and skittish. What kind of idiot am I to trust a boy I met at a diner? And why? Because he is cute and his gray-with-blue-flecks eyes look at me in a way I've always wanted to be looked at? Because we both knew the same physics joke?

"I think you need to drive me home," I say, ignoring the sparklers low in my belly when he rubs his thumb over his lower lip. Max's lower lip, by the way, is my favorite of the two. It is full and nicely curved and just the tiniest bit chapped.

"But we haven't found Paris," Max says, voice lifting like it's a question.

"Home," I repeat. "Please."

He hesitates, although I don't know why. She's not his sister.

"Okay," Max says eventually. "Whatever you want, Leo."

As we pull up to my house, Max says, "I'll wait for you."

But I tell him, "No."

My heart is hammering.

The Mazda is not parked in our driveway and neither is Mom's car or Tommy's Tahoe. I can tell by the angle of the blinds in my mother's bedroom at the front of the house that she's gone out. When she's gone she always lifts them just a little because she thinks it makes it look like someone's home.

Is she out looking for my sister? Or just out?

I want Max to stay.

Only that's not going to happen.

I am not a girl in some mystery movie. I am Leo Hollings, and later this morning I will put on my heinous-looking Yogiberry uniform and serve frozen yogurt and explain topping choices to people incapable of reading the labels on the containers.

So I will go inside, and Max will go back to his life and his own secrets—which I will not ever know.

"You've done enough," I tell him. "There's nothing else you can do."

Still, when Max scrawls his cell number on the back of a flimsy white napkin, I take it from him.

"Call me," he says. "Let me know what happens."

I don't turn around when I walk up the driveway, but not because I don't want to.

TEN

ALONE IN OUR HOUSE, I DO A QUICK TOUR—PARIS'S ROOM LOOKS THE same as before—then in the kitchen, I pour myself a huge glass of water and drink most of it. I start a pot of coffee. It's too late to sleep.

Tommy's whiskey glass is in the sink now, and the kitchen table is wiped up. The pantry door is hanging open, the garbage can lid half off. A crust of toast sits on the kitchen counter, but there's no other evidence of a meal. Did Tommy come back and they went to breakfast?

Then I see it: a note from my mother in messy, slanted cursive, tucked under the toast plate.

She was supposed to call Max's cell!

My heart drums in my ears.

But she's written only: *Paris—if you read this, call me immediately. Leo—if you read this, stay put till I get back.*

The knot between my shoulder blades loosens, just slightly.

At least she's doing something, which is more than I can say for her lately.

The note doesn't mention Tommy. Has she talked to him? Where did he go?

I wash the dishes while the coffee finishes, then pour a mug and carry it to my room. The routine calms me, but only a little. The house feels oddly empty and this bumps my pulse again.

If something has actually happened to Paris, would I know? People say that sometimes, don't they? *I knew something was wrong. I had a feeling.*

Probably I don't need the caffeine. I'm wired enough as it is.

In the bathroom, door locked even though I'm alone, I stand in the shower until the water—its spray intermittent because the showerhead's broken—is lukewarm and heading toward cold.

I do not think about Max. Not for long, anyway. Probably he is not thinking about me, either. If he is, he's wondering why I stopped this whole thing in the middle. Why I made him take me home. Why my sister is such a screwball.

And I am wondering why I somehow feel responsible for it all.

I look at Paris's notes again. I change into shorts and my

favorite black tank, the soft cotton one that looks good on me. I go online and leave messages everywhere I think she might check, but still nothing, which does not surprise me.

I leaf randomly through my SAT prep book. Calculate five pages of algebra problems I could do in my sleep.

Max's phone number sits on the scrap of napkin. Even scribbled, his handwriting has an evenness to it, the lines and curves clearly defined. But it's not like I'm going to talk to him again.

When all this does not take away the swirly feeling inside me, I lay my head on my pillow, its smooth white case dotted with tiny wildflowers, and close my eyes. But my stomach keeps flipping, and I end up with one foot on the floor like I've done the few times I've had too much to drink and the room is spinning.

Only when a clanking noise wakes me—heart pounding, mouth sticky yet dry, which means that maybe it was hanging open—do I realize I've fallen asleep, a deep dreamless sleep, the kind that feels like smothering.

I stumble up and cross the hall.

"Paris?"

But she's not in her room, just all that scattered stuff that isn't like her. I sit down on the could-be-cleaner rug and pick up one of her black boots. She's glued the sole back on where it cracked. Vegas heat is hell on cheap shoes.

Something new catches my eye, poking from under the dust ruffle. It's a postcard of the Hollywood sign in LA, probably something Paris was going to use in a collage. She uses old postcards a lot, finds them in thrift stores. I turn it over. She's written the name Toby on the back in thin black ink.

Does it mean something? Has she run off with this boy I've never met? Or worse, has he made her go somehow? Or is it just random as everything else in our life—things that happen and then you're stuck with them, can't make them disappear no matter how much you try.

I look at my sister's precise, even script and wonder, not for the first time, if you can ever really know someone— deep down at that molecular level. Ever really understand what makes someone tick. Maybe you can't. Maybe the truth is that we're all in this alone.

The thought deflates me, and I lean back against Paris's bed. Ponder that last note, the one from the top of the Stratosphere. *We were happy, right?* And that part about being near the water.

It makes as much sense as everything else tonight, which is to say: not much. We used to live in LA. Everything was near the water, more or less.

Were we happy there?

Sometimes.

Like the day Paris and I wandered this flea market in Venice and I found Tiny Tim on a table next to a pile of Coach knockoffs and she found this red leather wallet with a plastic strip of pictures of people we didn't know. At home later, she cut their faces out with a small, pointy silver scissors so she could use them in her art: a middle-aged man in a suit and tie; an old lady wearing a white wool hat with a pom-pom on top; two kids—a boy and girl—standing on the edge of the ocean. Which I thought looked weird.

But we were laughing, and she pasted the lady with the pom-pom onto the upper branches of this tree she'd drawn with charcoal pencils and I dusted off Tiny Tim's bony clavicle, and it was one of the moments you have with the people you love where you don't need to explain how you are. They just know.

If that was happy, then we were.

But so what?

My gaze drifts over the bracelets, beads, and shoes scattered around me. I smell traces of hot glue gun lingering in the air. Then the door creaks and Tommy Davis—wearing tight-fitting cowboy-type jeans, a Harley T-shirt, and brown lace-up John Deere boots—stomps into the room.

I jump.

"Where's your sister?" he asks, standing over me.

I hoist myself off the floor, leaping up so fast that my feet feel momentarily unsteady. Tommy reaches out a hand, grips my arm. I see my mother's name, Callie, tattooed on the inside of his wrist, the final *e* twisting up at the end.

"I'm fine," I say, and he lets go, then waves Mom's note at me, and it slips from his fingers, fluttering to the floor next to Paris's boots. There's a hint of liquor on his breath still.

"Why's your mother out looking for Paris?"

"She ditched me," I say, trying to sound casual about it. "Paris. At a diner. She went out to the car and didn't come back. She's not answering her cell, either." I hesitate, and when his face remains neutral I add, "You know Paris. It's just one of her . . . things. She left me a note. Like some game or something."

Tommy scrapes his teeth over his lower lip. He shakes his head. "Your sister is a pain in the ass sometimes, isn't she?"

I frown. "She's not your business, Tommy. I'll take care of it."

I wait for him to get pissed off, the way he does when Paris or I tell him to mind his own business, but instead he asks, "You want to drive around looking for her? I'll take you, Leo. Your mother won't be out there much longer. You know her." He taps his jeans pocket and his keys jingle. "C'mon," he says. "Go for doughnuts while we're at it. You like that Devil Doughnuts place, right? They're probably putting out the first ones right now." He fishes the keys from his pocket with two fingers.

"Maybe," I say, even though I mean no. I start toward the door. I don't like him in Paris's room, her space.

He rests a hand on my shoulder. "So what were you two

up to out there?" he asks, conversational about it. "What diner? You go anywhere else?"

I shrug, but his hand stays put. "Around. You know." I take another step. His hand slides off.

"I made coffee," I say. "You see it?" I had been tired, but now I am fully awake.

"Your sister is eighteen," Tommy says, not commenting on the coffee. "She can do what she wants, Leo."

I walk another few steps, weaving my way around all the crap and shoes on the floor. He follows.

"Leo." He pauses, and there is something about the absence of sound that makes me turn. "How'd you get home?"

It takes me a beat too long to work up the lie. "Cab," I say. "Thanks for the mad money." The phrase was awkward sounding when he said it, even worse when I do. In my head I see that crumpled bill riding the breeze over Paradise Road. It's a dumb lie. My mother *met* Max.

Tommy glances around, then back to me.

"What are you doing in here anyway?" he says, like he suddenly finds it strange I'd be in my sister's room. "You know how she is about people touching her shit."

We stand there for a few long beats.

"You two picking up guys?" he asks. His voice lowers. "Is that where she is, off with some guy?"

"No!" I say, voice sharp. In my head, I think of Max Sullivan, who I told to get lost.

"Chill, Leonora," Tommy says. "You sure do get worked up about things." He runs his hand lightly down my arm.

"Don't," I say.

"You back there, Tommy?" calls my mother's voice—tired and annoyed sounding—from the other end of our skinny hallway. "Where the hell have you been? I come home after a double shift and there's Leo with—"

She stops talking as she walks into the room, face pinched and pale. Her eyes fix on Tommy. On his hand, resting at the top of my wrist.

"How long have you two been home?" she asks, voice tight.

Tommy takes his hand away.

"Did you find Paris?" I ask, even though it's clear she hasn't. She's wearing a sleeveless turquoise shirt with a scoop neck and the skin at her collarbone looks red and blotchy. Her black yoga shorts are stretched tightly over her thighs.

Mom crosses her arms. Her fake nails are growing out and I can see the half-moons of her pale cuticles. "I drove around," she says, "to that dance club in Henderson your sister goes to even though she thinks I don't know about it."

I stare at her, startled. She pays like zero attention to what we do. But somehow she knows this.

"And where have you been this whole time, Leonora?" she asks, even though she knows full well she told me to deal with it. "Where's that boy?"

"Boy?" Tommy's brows lift. "What boy?"

"No one," I say. "It's—we . . . I found another note," I correct, pulse thrumming. "I don't know what it means. I don't know where she is." I force myself to breathe slowly. "Maybe we should call the cops."

"We don't need the cops." Tommy's voice lazes out. He rubs his nose with the back of his hand. "Your sister knows how to take care of herself. She'll be back when she's back. I don't know what you two are so hysterical about."

"You been drinking?" Mom's gaze cuts to Tommy. Her voice sharpens dangerously.

"I can handle it," he says, shrugging, hands palms up. Then to me: "You make this mess in here? You know your sister likes things just so."

Is he serious?

He stoops slowly, making a production of it, picks up Paris's black boots and sets them neatly together at the foot of her bed.

My mother says nothing.

"Mom," I say. "We need to do something. Maybe something happened." The thought makes my throat feel hollow.

"Nothing happened," Tommy says.

"How the hell do you know?"

"Watch your mouth, Leo," Mom snaps.

Tommy Davis looks me square in the eyes, not blinking.

The flush on my mother's chest rushes up her neck to the roots of her hair.

"Leonora." Mom runs her gaze over me, something in her eyes that I can't read. "I told you before. Your sister is a drama queen. I'm sure she's fine."

"Then why did you go out looking for her? Why aren't you asleep?" My voice spikes, and Mom's eyes momentarily widen.

"Don't yell at your mother," Tommy says. "Jesus, Leo." He lifts his hands like I'm robbing him. "Calm the hell down."

My mind flashes briefly to Max, standing with me on the roof of the Stratosphere, shoving asshole Nate.

"Fuck you," I say.

"Go to your room!" Mom screams.

Our eyes lock, this same woman who used to take us for picnics on the beach at Santa Monica. My mother, who always said hello to the white statue of Saint Monica that stands above the beach not far from Wilshire. "Hey, Mon," she'd call breezily. "How's the saint business going?" She'd run her hand over Saint Monica's feet, then take us to the pier for hot, greasy churros.

Now my mother drops her gaze. "Go to your room, Leo. Please."

Door closed, my desk chair under the handle because nothing actually works in this house and even if I click the lock button the knob turns if you jiggle the handle—I sit on my bed, hand pressed to my knees, listening. Waiting for her to tell him that her girls are her business and not his, which she has told him before.

But I hear them walk away, then the clanging of dishes in the kitchen and then nothing, which means they've gone to their room, and I'm left with the sound of my too-fast breathing. Hot, angry tears rush from my eyes.

It is edging past nine in the morning. The sun is shining outside my window, the desert heat attempting to muscle its way in. Yesterday it was 106 degrees. In the summer it hardly ever rains. It didn't rain much in LA, either. But there was the ocean. I see it in my mind again, over the shoulders of the sparkling white statue of Saint Monica, past the wide expanse of beach.

I stand. I pace, walking in circles until, lacking any better idea, I sink cross-legged in front of my old dollhouse with its garish multicolored rooms, remembering how I'd worried earlier that Max would make fun of it. Because I'm seventeen, not seven.

But I love that house, probably more than I've ever loved any of the places we've lived, any of the real rooms I've made my own. And the dolls that Paris helped me make for it, recycling old cheap plastic dolls and doing up their hair and finding outfits for them to wear: one that was supposed to be me, dressed in jeans and a red shirt and this tiny dorky white cardigan that she'd found at a resale shop on Melrose. She'd stitched *Leo* on it in pretty yellow thread with this silly smiley-face underneath, all so tiny that I had no idea how she'd done it. We'd placed it in the pink-decorated bedroom and—after a brief debate on which color best reflected each of us—disregarded all logic on that issue and declared it the Leo room.

The Paris doll had lighter hair and a tiny bracelet on its skinny plastic wrist and redder lips that Paris had painted in an oil paint that even all these years later hadn't chipped. We gave that doll the bedroom we painted red like those lips.

My sister and I played with that house for a long time. No matter where we landed as our mother bounced us from place to place, the dollhouse stayed the same. Each time we'd move, I'd set it up exactly, each doll and piece of furniture precisely as it had been.

Without meaning to, my mind drifts to Max. Is he sleeping? Is his hair still sticking out, that one strand still curling down by his neck?

And then I see the dolls.

The Paris doll isn't in its red bedroom anymore. Instead, it's propped into the little rocking chair near the fireplace in my pink room. The Leo sweater doll is resting on the cute four-poster bed that I always wished was mine in real life.

The rocking chair—which I had angled toward the fireplace—is now turned to the mini four-poster bed, the Paris doll propped in it, facing the Leo doll—almost like it's guarding it.

And then my eyes go wide. In the red Paris room, a

piece of paper sits on the tiny white wooden chest of draw-
ers. I pick it up and read the message in minuscule but
distinctly Paris script:

> You need to leave this house, Leo. You
> need to find me. Now.

I read it over and over, breath freezing in my lungs.

One thought repeats: not a game. Something has happened to Paris. But what?

My hands shake as I stand and walk to my closet,
thoughts flying, heart pounding. I open the door, half
expecting Paris to be crouched in there, hiding. Once she'd
waited an entire day until I opened our refrigerator and
screamed my head off because she'd placed her old rubber
Frankenstein head from Halloween in there.

But she's not here. Of course she's not here. The fear
returns and tightens.

I have to find her. I have to go now. Do I tell Mom? Will
she believe me? Will she care? The words of this new note
sear into me. *You need to leave this house, Leo. You need to
find me. Now.*

I rush to the back of the closet, stretch up, and reach
behind folded blankets for the box. My fingers touch it,
tapping it closer until I can slide it forward and wrap my
hand around the raggedy cigar box I'd decorated with
smiley-face stickers back in third grade.

My breath catches as I open the lid, expecting to see my old green pencil bag, the one that holds the fat wad of rubber-banded bills: $5,780 in twenties and tens and fives and ones. Lots of ones because we have a tip jar at Yogiberry and at the end of each week we split the proceeds. My entire life savings. Not much of a hiding place, but who would ever look up there but me?

But the box is too light now, and I know before I see it what I'm going to find.

It's gone. All of it. Every single bill. Every single dollar. Just an empty box.

Well, not completely empty.

Inside, smiley-face stickered to the white bottom, sits one other note.

Find me. I've got your money safe, but I need you, L. xoParis

ELEVEN

I HAVE NO IDEA WHERE MAX LIVES, BUT I HAVEN'T BEEN SITTING ON THE park swing for long when he pulls up. My heart is drumming, and my back is clammy with sweat under my tank top, and I keep glancing down the street, more than half expecting Mom or Tommy to be striding toward me. But no one comes except Max.

He doesn't ask. He doesn't say anything, not even "How are you?" The first thing Max does is this: he wraps his arms around me and holds me tight. His face is very, very close and he smells like night air and heat. I do not push him away.

We sit like this for a while, not saying anything. The notes from the dollhouse and the cigar box are clutched in my hand. My heart is beating insanely fast.

Max holds me until it slows down.

Then I explain. At least the parts I can.

"I have to tell it from the beginning," I say. "Is that okay?"

He makes a face at the last part, like this is a silly thing to say. I follow him to a molded plastic bench a few feet away. "From the beginning," he says.

I tell him. The dollhouse, the notes, the money.

"It's gone," I squeak eventually. "All of it. Every single dollar." I can't tell him the number. I just can't.

"I'm so stupid," I say. "God."

Max's gaze does not leave me as I talk. His frown is very deep. We sit on the bench and he studies the scrap of lined spiral notebook paper from all angles, as though this is going to change what it says. He brushes his finger over the shreds of ripped spiral on its side.

On a shaky breath, I say, "She has my life savings. My college money."

He's silent for so long I think that maybe he doesn't believe me.

Then he smiles tightly and says, "Guess she wants to make sure you come after her, huh?"

I nod mutely.

"Don't worry. We'll figure it out, though, okay?"

It's the "we" that calms me down. Or maybe just how his voice is deep and even as he says it.

"Okay," I say, nodding. My heart slows to a normal person's.

We sit together some more, and I hold on to what I didn't tell Max, don't tell him even now: how after I stepped from the closet, I started for the door. Decided I would tell my mother. I hated her now for many reasons, but she needed to know this, right? That Paris had taken my hidden cash and was maybe gone for real, maybe in trouble or hurt or . . . who the hell knew what. Shaking, I walked down the hall.

From the other side of the house as I neared the kitchen, I heard Tommy's voice rise again and my mother's in response. She laughed, low and throaty. Floorboards creaked. More laughing.

"Love you," I heard my mother say through the thin walls of our no-privacy house.

It was not the words that made me change my mind. It was the light, girlish sound and pitch of her voice. I knew in the pit of my stomach that if I knocked on their door, she would tell me to figure it out myself.

I waited. One second. Two. Three. At ten, I walked into the kitchen. I unzipped my mother's purse. From her wallet, I took four twenty-dollar bills, leaving her three. On the rare occasions I sneak money from my mother's wallet, I always leave some behind so she doesn't notice right away. So she thinks maybe she spent it and just forgot.

My hand hesitated over her cell phone, but only briefly. I took that, too.

On the top of a small stack of yellow Post-its resting by

the stove, I wrote: *Gone to find Paris.* My hand shook and my heart was beating in my ears, but my mother had sided with Tommy Davis. Was always going to side with him. What else was there to say?

Out on the street, I walked around the corner and then another full block before I used Mom's cell, pressing in the numbers I had memorized even though Max had written them down for me.

He'd answered on the third ring, his voice full of sleep, then instantly alert when I said his name.

"Leo. Are you okay? Did Paris come home?"

"No."

I was crying then, even though I do not cry in front of boys or anyone, but the more I tried to stop, the more the tears came. Why had I called him? I should hang up.

"Where are you?" Max asked.

"I'm sorry I bothered you. I— Don't worry."

"Where are you, Leo?" In the silence that followed, I heard him breathing.

Two blocks down from our house is a little park with a bench and a swing and a plastic jungle gym that's always too hot to touch and a patch of pebbles and weeds that used to be grass.

I hesitated. He stayed silent with me, but somehow I could hear him waiting. I told him where I was.

"I'll be right there," said Max Sullivan, the boy I've

known for less than a day. "Stay put."

"I'm fine. Really. I just . . ."

But he'd already hung up.

"So here's the thing," Max says. We're in the Ranger now, engine cranked and idling. We have come up with no particular plan on how to make my sister reappear. "I have to go to work for a few hours."

"Shit," I say, and Max cocks his head. "Me, too. Work, I mean." My hands flutter up for emphasis, and knock into a little Christmas-tree-shaped air freshener dangling from the rearview mirror along with his museum hangtags.

I tap the tree again with my finger, and when I glance over at Max, he's blushing.

"It's supposed to get rid of the French fry smell."

"It's working." Actually, it's added fake pine smell to stale fast food, but I decide this is one of those cases where it's the thought that counts.

I call in sick to work, to which I am already late. Kyle threatens to fire me and I say go ahead and he says fine and then hangs up. My stomach bunches into knots—I need this job. I need the money. But I tell myself that the fake pine air freshener smells better than most of the frozen yogurt at Yogiberry. Probably tastes better, too. I will remember this when I'm groveling to get my job back tomorrow.

"Frozen yogurt, huh?"

"Queen of the dessert industry. That's me." I smile as brightly as possible. "My parfaits are killer. Absolutely."

Max explains that he has two tours to conduct: a mini talk about extraterrestrials with a group coming to the Area 51 exhibit.

"Hey," he says when I giggle. "This is serious stuff."

He pretends to look offended, and as he shoves the truck in gear, I realize what I haven't said.

"Thank you for coming," I tell him. I blink, hard, when my eyes fill with tears.

"It'll be okay," Max says, using that word again. "I bet by the time I give my tours, your sister will be home. You'll see. And don't stress about the money. She's got it. You know that, right?"

He says it like it's absolutely true, or maybe like people do when they've never had to worry about money. His optimism should annoy me. I am not a fan of overly cheerful, positive people. I always figure they have something to hide. But somehow with Max, it doesn't bother me at all.

We pull into the parking lot of the Atomic Testing Museum. Paris is still not answering her cell.

Max untangles his name tag on its little blue lanyard from the air freshener and pulls it over his head. He's wearing khakis again, and a different blue button-down that gives a slightly blue cast to his gray eyes.

Max Sullivan/Tour Guide and I step into the heat and

then into the artificial cool of the museum.

"Do you know there were over one thousand nuclear tests in Nevada?" he says as the door closes behind us. "Crazy, right?"

"Hmm," I say. I rub my arms.

"Wanna see the Ground Zero film?"

This is *not,* it turns out once Max settles me onto a hard little bench in the front row of the darkened auditorium, about September 11. It's actual documentary footage of the nuclear bomb the government tested at the Bikini Atoll in the Pacific. The benches vibrate and the light strobes and a huge wind rushes from the vents when the mushroom cloud rises.

I watch it three times while Max works.

After that, I walk around.

Max is leading a group of day camp kids, all with matching blue T-shirts that say *Heinrich YMCA Summers Rock!* over to the special exhibit on Area 51. "We don't normally allow tour groups in here," he tells them in a loud, conspiratorial-sounding voice. "But I'm going to let you see anyway." And in they go.

I trail behind, listening as Max explains about Area 51 and aliens and UFOs and secrets and waves his hands in the air every time he says the word *secret,* in a very scary-sounding voice. The kids cluster tight around him like he's the most interesting person they've ever met.

Max keeps his face absolutely serious, even when a little

girl asks if he's ever seen an alien. "Maybe," he tells her, and her eyes go wide. I cover my mouth so I won't laugh and ruin the moment.

"Who's she?" asks a boy with tight dreadlocks. He points to me. "You work here, too?"

"Don't mess with her, dude. She's got her own skeleton. She knows all the bones in the human body."

I blush, right up to the roots of my hair.

"Are you a scientist?" the boys asks.

This takes me by surprise. So does my honest answer. "I, uh . . . I'm going to be a doctor. So I can help people when they get sick." I wonder if I say it aloud enough, I will figure out a way to make it true.

"Science is serious." Dreadlock boy glances at Max as if to confirm this.

"Two atoms bump into each other," Max says with a straight face. "One says, 'I lost an electron!' The other asks him, 'Are you sure?' And the first atom replies, 'I'm positive.'"

I leave them to discuss why this is funny.

In front of the exhibit that tracks active radiation in the state of Nevada, I check Mom's phone again.

Eight missed calls, all from Tommy's phone. Also a message.

I decide that it's just my mother calling her phone, trying to find it.

Mom's voice shoots shrilly into my ear. "Where the hell are you, Leo? I know you have my phone." Then there's a shuffling and I hear Tommy's voice say something I can't make out and then, softer, my mother says: "Honey. Leo. Come home. Please. We'll find Paris. But I need you here. I need to know you're safe. You're with that boy, aren't you?"

I hear Tommy again, muttering something about how they should have put that tracker program on Mom's phone.

I press delete.

In the exhibit area, I check the radiation levels for Las Vegas and Henderson and a few other places while my pulse stops pinballing.

Although the levels of gamma radiation are currently okay, it is entirely possible that at some point they were not.

No wonder the museum is mostly empty except for Max's groups.

"My mom took me here last year," says a voice, and I jump. It's dreadlock boy, separated from the herd. He frowns at the charts. "She says a bunch of actors got cancer because they were filming movies in the desert near the testing."

"Well," I say. "That was a long time ago." He does not look comforted. I am seriously bad with kids. "That's why they check now," I tell him, making it up as I go along. "Every Tuesday afternoon, like clockwork."

"Sometimes Wednesdays," says Max from behind me.

My ears go hot. How long has he been standing there?

"You Noah?" Max says to the boy.

"Yeah." Noah stares up at Max. "You're tall."

"You're late. You want the bus to leave without you?"

Noah considers this. "Maybe," he says.

"People would miss you," I say. "They'd be worried you got lost." I nudge my foot against Noah's sneaker.

Noah considers this.

"Nah," he says. "I'm not lost." He looks confident and happy, the way kids do when they believe nothing in this world can ever actually hurt them.

Max escorts Noah to the exit.

Maybe it's watching him bounce happily at Max's side. Maybe it's just the odd way things come to you when you're not expecting them.

She'd been trying to tell me, hadn't she? I smack the heel of my hand against my forehead, like in a cartoon. All I need is one of those thought bubbles.

In my head, I see our little apartment in Santa Monica. The last place we were ever happy in the way people want to be happy. Even if the bills weren't getting paid on time and the carpet in the family room had a burned spot in the corner where a previous tenant had dropped a cigarette and the landlord hadn't replaced it.

Noah, dreadlocks bouncing, climbs onto the bus.

Max strides back to me, arms swinging cheerfully at his sides.

"Hey," he says like he's been gone awhile.

"LA," I say. Adrenaline punches through me. The fear eases its grip.

"Huh?" Max tilts his head.

"Paris is in LA. I need to go to LA, Max. She's there."

My sister is not just dicking around Vegas driving me crazy. Not just disappeared without me, either. If she ran away, my sister would *never* take my stuff with her. Never leave me . . . no.

Something's happened. She needs me. And yeah, her method of delivery needs some work, but we can discuss that once I've found her.

A curious expression crosses Max's face, lingering just behind those gray eyes. "You really think so?" He's not doubting me, just asking.

"Yeah," I say. I make him read the notes again. I jab my finger to the one taped on the railing of the Stratosphere, pointing to the word *happy*.

"I didn't think she'd be so obvious about it," I say. "I mean, that part's not like her. Paris usually dances around stuff, but I guess not this time. I know it's crazy, right? But I don't know what else it could be. I don't know where else she'd go but there."

He doesn't look convinced—which I get. He is a scientist, like me. He needs a context.

But how do I explain how my sister feels about LA? I would have to tell him about that red wallet with its pictures of strangers that Paris turned into something new. How she took people who'd been discarded or lost and made them into art. How when she had finished, she sat there looking so satisfied at what she had created. And that when, not long after that, our mother announced that we were leaving LA and moving to Vegas with Tommy Davis, Paris decided to leave the pictures on the wall in her room in our Santa Monica apartment. The one with the window that faced the ocean—at least if you hung your head out and craned your neck.

If she were really in trouble, I think she'd feel safe there. Familiar.

But why not tell me? Why just take my money and run?

I have no choice but to find her. Maybe that's the point.

But even as I try to put all this in words, Max's face curves into yet another bright smile.

"Then I guess we're headed to LA," he declares.

My heart and pulse rocket off to unknown heights. He can't really mean it. Who would do this for a person he barely knows?

"You don't have to come with me. I get if you can't—"

"I can," Max says. "If you want me to. When my shift is over. Do you want me to go with you, Leo?" He looks at me intently, holding my gaze tight until finally I'm the one who looks away.

I try to work it out like an equation. Me plus boy I don't know plus missing sister plus road trip . . . but the unknown throws me, and I don't know how to solve for it.

Max is silent, waiting.

Everything that has happened swells around me, also waiting.

I swallow. Breathe through my nose.

"Yeah," I tell Max.

"Yeah you're going? Or yeah I'm going with you?"

"Both?" I leave it a question.

"Both." Max makes it a statement.

TWELVE

"WHEN WAS THE LAST TIME YOU SLEPT?" THIS IS WHAT MAX ASKS WHEN the last of his second tour group marches out the front door. I'm sitting on a wooden bench in the lobby, the items in the museum gift shop, including the Albert Einstein bobble-head, having occupied me for only so long.

I stare at him, yawning. "Not tired," I lie. I yawn again.

"You can sleep on the way," Max says, sounding peppy. "I'll drive."

Well, of course he'll drive. It's his truck. The plan sounds perfect . . . for like three seconds. Then reality hits. I have known Max for less than a day. Do I really want to sack out in his truck while he drives for hours through the desert?

I tell him as much. His forehead creases. I observe that he could probably use some sleep, too. The last thing we need to do is drift off and crash in the desert. I do not add the following:

now that he has fumigated the Ranger, we wouldn't even have fast-food refuse to snack on until help came.

When I'm done talking, Max says he agrees.

This poses another problem: me plus boy I don't know plus napping.

"I'm not going home until I find Paris," I say, brushing my bangs with my fingers.

"I get that. We can crash at my place. Then we'll go."

Max is a very smart and gainfully employed Atomic Testing Museum worker. But poker players are poker players.

Even poker players who know physics. I am not going home with him.

"Well," I say, and stop. Maybe we can just curl up in the Area 51 exhibit.

Max shoves a hand through his wild hair. "I'll call Nate."

"Nate? Stratosphere Nate?" Is he insane?

"He also works valet at the Luxor."

"So?"

"So he has connections. C'mon," he says, tugging my hand. I dig in my heels. "You'll see. Trust me," he adds when I hold my ground. "Really."

As if to seal the deal, he disappears briefly into the gift shop and returns with a souvenir T-shirt, the one with a mushroom cloud and the words *Have a Blast*.

"Really?" I say as he hands it to me.

He grins. "It's our best seller."

* * *

The Luxor Hotel is a huge fake pyramid, rising from the concrete desert, a giant fake Sphinx guarding its front. At night, a huge blue beacon shoots up into the sky from the top of the pyramid, like a lighthouse for lost sailors.

Only this is Vegas. The Luxor light guides people headed up I-15 from the coast to a casino designed to take their money.

We valet the truck. Nate, it turns out, is not the only Luxor employee in Max's acquaintance. The valet guy—chubbier than Nate and older—hands Max a room key card in its little holder and tells him that he should drop it off when we pick up the car.

"You know a lot of people." People who hook you up with hotel rooms that don't require checking in at the desk.

Max shrugs, looking away then back to me. He's holding the bag of In-N-Out Burger we picked up on the way, and I can smell the grease from the burgers and fries.

He pulls a small duffel bag from behind the driver's seat.

"Clothes," he says when I eye the duffel. Does he keep the bag there all the time? Is Max Sullivan always prepared for impromptu road trips? And why is it—really—that he's not in college, but here, guiding tours at the Atomic Testing Museum and eating at the Heartbreak and playing poker with guys like Nate?

He has volunteered to drive me to LA. Is this enough to trust him?

There is only one person I trust completely. And she is currently missing.

We leave the heat and walk inside. The cavernous hotel makes me half dizzy—because it's a pyramid, everything in the Luxor is on an angle. Even here in the lobby where it's not quite as obvious.

The entire place is aggressively artificial. Suddenly I need to hear something from Max that feels true and real.

"What's your story?" I study him in the dim light, watch his eyes flicker with all sorts of things, possibly even the truth.

"Why are you here? Not here"—I gesture with one hand to the Luxor lobby—"but in Vegas."

He doesn't answer right away. A girl a little older than me, in six-inch red stilettos, teeters by, dragging a multi-colored wheeled carry-on bag.

"Leo," Max says slowly. He swallows. I watch his Adam's apple bob. The hotel angles around us.

"I . . . things were bad for me in Texas. So I left for a while. But I'm going back to college. At least that's the plan." He pauses, biting his lower lip. "Biology," he says, holding my gaze. "I'm going to narrow it down once I get there. Biophysics, maybe, since I like physics, too. Or bio-chemistry. I think I'd like to do research. Or maybe end up an engineer. There's a lot of possibilities."

He sounds so confident that it will all work out. But he's not a kid like that boy Noah at the museum. A million questions rise to my tongue, including what he would research, but I hold them back.

"So not premed like Nate, right?" I say instead, arching my eyebrows. There's a pause and then Max laughs.

"Nate," says Max Sullivan, "is a shithead who nevertheless helped us get a room to crash in. A big room," he adds, neck reddening, but so slightly I might have missed it. "With more than one bed."

We're silent for longer than feels comfortable, and so I say, "I'm going to Stanford if I get in, then med school." Max is not the only one who can fake confidence in his life plans.

"Physics major?" Max grins.

How did he . . . Oh. My first words to him were a physics joke.

"But you're just a senior, right?" he adds.

Is it that obvious?

I nod, feel awkward. "I want to be a doctor," I say, trying to sound focused and older. Not like the girl whose college fund—which probably is only enough to pay for a year of textbooks—has gone missing with her sister. "My SATs are high, but I'm going to take them again. I need to up my verbal scores mostly. Not that they're low. Just that it could always be higher, you know. For Stanford."

I trail off because how much of the painfully obvious can I spout here? Max looks like he might say more, but he adds only, "It's all good, Leo Leonora."

He holds out his hand, and after a few beats I extend mine. We shake, warm palms pressed together. I don't know what we're agreeing to.

* * *

Elevator, I discover, is not an accurate term here in fake Egypt. At the Luxor they are called *inclinators* because they haul you up the pyramid on an angle steep enough that somewhere as we rise to Floor 25, I stumble as it jolts sideways and Max grabs my arm so I don't fall.

Our room has a slanted window. I know this because I smack my head as I lean to check out the view.

After that, we make the following plan: We will eat our burgers. We will nap. Around six as it gets cooler, we'll head out, driving west as the sun sets. If there's no traffic, we'll make it to LA before midnight.

This is the plan Max and I make as we sit at the little table near the window where I just hit my head hard enough to raise a lump on my temple. I nibble a fry from the pile we're sharing and begin to wonder if any of this makes sense at all.

Maybe I should just go home. Max will go wherever Max needs to go. If Paris doesn't show up, I will go to the police and drag my mother with me. We'll report my sister missing. Maybe they'll do something.

But my eyes are drooping again and my belly is full of grease and I flop down on the bed nearest the door, setting my Diet Coke on the nightstand.

"Leo," Max says, his voice tired sounding and low. He closes the drapes, but not all the way, so there's this little gap of light in the gloom, and he stretches out on the other bed, arms behind his head. "Don't worry, okay?"

"Not worried," I lie.

"Tell me more about you," he says, and my pulse skips. It is not the question I expected.

"Like what?"

His voice rises in the darkened room. "Like more than Stanford. Things you like. Things you hate. Stuff. You know."

It feels like a test. Or a job interview. Or maybe it's because I don't talk to guys much. And guys like Buddy Lathrop aren't interested in knowing stuff about you.

"I hate frozen yogurt." If the floor opened up right now and swallowed me, that would be a good thing. I am glad it is dark and we are not looking at each other. I imagine if we were, his gray eyes would be laughing.

"Oh," says Max, but the gentle upturn of his voice encourages me to continue down yogurt lane even as the sensible part of my brain is shouting, *God. Please. Stop.*

"There are exactly three types of frozen yogurt eaters, you know," I tell him, counting off on my fingers. "The ones who eat it because they think it's healthy, which if they ever really thought about it, they would know it's just big vats of chemicals with a hint of milk product. Then there's the subgroup of that—the ones who tell themselves it's health food and therefore they can eat like a trough of the crap. You can get as many toppings as fit in the cup. So they ask for blueberries and chocolate and cereal and even that mochi stuff."

"That stuff that tastes like pencil eraser?"

I smile. "Yeah."

"What the hell is that, anyway?"

"Nobody knows. It's part of the appeal."

"You have a finely honed set of yogurt factoids, Leo Leonora."

I think about telling him to stop calling me that. Then I think maybe I like it and keep my mouth shut.

"And the third type of person?"

"You don't really want to know."

"I absolutely do," he says, and he sounds like he means it.

"Well," I say, trying for dramatic.

"Worse than topping hoarders?"

"Maybe. It's the guys on dates. We're down the block from the Cinemark, you know. So guys bring their dates in for dessert. And you know they're just pretending to like the stuff because . . . well, they're just pretending. Because what boy walks into Yogiberry on his own? No one's like, 'Hey, the heck with hot wings, I want frozen chemicals in a cup with fruit topping.'"

Max snorts a laugh. A rustling sound, and in the near darkness, I see him sit up.

"But they think the girl's going to like it, right? So you're saying that's bad?"

I feel myself blush, hope he can't see. "I'm saying they probably hate it. So here you are on a date and you're eating something you despise, only if the girl is honest, she probably doesn't want it either. But she's eating it because that's what girls do, you know?"

"What?" he asks when I don't finish. When I clam up because, for the love of God, how insanely boring am I?

"Doesn't matter," I mutter. "It's yogurt."

The heat in my face has spread to my neck. He's going to think I am anti-date. Or anti-romance. Or anti-dessert, which I am not, but would be the least bad of the lot.

And then he says quietly, "You're saying people lie to each other. Even about yogurt."

Which is when I understand that this is exactly what I'm saying. To this boy I still barely know.

Maybe the truth is easier with people we barely know.

"I like avocados," I say, just throwing it out there. "And old-school video games. And the beach. Also the mountains but not as much. Sliced tomatoes but not those little cherry ones. And breakfast. I'm a fan of breakfast. Especially waffles. And zombie movies, but I guess that goes without saying."

"Of course."

And because I don't know where to go after that, I ask instead, "Do you miss Texas?"

There are two types of silence, one peaceful, the other not, and this time Max's silence is of the second variety.

"Sometimes," he says. "Yeah. Sometimes a lot. I was surprised. Houston's not a place people line up to visit. But I grew up there. So yeah."

The sound of his voice is even and calm and my stomach stops plunging from what had moved without my permission from yogurt babble to personal. The worry about Paris scuttles into a corner. For now.

"What do you miss?" I ask, wanting more than anything right now for him to keep talking.

"There's this little grocery store a few blocks from where I grew up," Max says, his longing bouncing off the angled windows and around the fake Egyptian décor, more authentic than anything in the room. "It's been there since like the forties, maybe before that. If you live in my neighborhood, they actually let you run a tab and then send the bill to your house at the end of the month. When I was a kid, my buddies and I would ride our bikes and get Cokes or ice cream or candy and I would say, 'Put it on the Sullivan account,'" he says, shaking his head. "I thought it was the greatest thing in the world."

He drifts off, the silence surging back. "What kind of candy?" I ask.

"Pop Rocks," Max says immediately. His voice brightens in the darkness. "I used to eat packages of the stuff."

In my head I see the market and a little version of Max—still with crazy, stick-up hair—tossing a bunch of those thin black Pop Rocks packages on the counter and invoking the Sullivan account. Only here's what my brain keeps coming back to: He lived in the same house near that funky little store for his entire life until he came here.

Same house. Same store. Same parents, as far as I can tell. Probably he doesn't even think about this.

But here he is anyway, with me, running from whatever he's running from.

What happened in Max's world that was so bad that he left it behind?

Max is still talking about Pop Rocks. The notes and silver Sharpie messages float behind my eyes, and the crap in Paris's room and Tommy Davis running a finger down my arm and my mother looking at me and all the rest of it, mixed and jumbled, my brain sorting and sorting.

I usually don't let myself feel sad. I mean honestly, what's the point? Because really, no one wants to be around sad people, at least not for very long. I'm more of a "pick yourself up and get on with it" type of girl.

"Leo?" The sound of my name startles me. On the ceiling above me, a little security light blinks green.

"Leo?" Max says again. He eases off the bed and crosses the short distance between us.

My heart goes crazy.

"You're crying," Max says, and I realize that tears are trickling from the corners of my eyes.

"Keep talking," I say, the words catching in my throat, traitors to my attempt to pretend that I am not a whiny crybaby. "Pop Rocks, right?"

"What's wrong?" Max is sitting on the edge of my bed now. "Are you okay?"

Nothing is worse when you are not okay than someone asking if you are. Because suddenly you're even less okay just because they cared to ask.

"How could you leave all that?" I blurt. Max's face is pale in the tiny sliver of light. The shadows play on his jaw and cheekbones. I'm not the only sad person in this slanted-windowed room.

"Yeah, I know. Who would leave Pop Rocks, right?"

He doesn't explain, and I don't ask him to.

Instead, he clicks on the lamp, a warm golden glow that breaks the gloom, and opens the drawer of the nightstand.

"Bible?" I say, wondering. But this is Vegas. He extracts a deck of cards and, with a flourish of his fingers, starts to shuffle it.

He doesn't ask if I want to play, just begins dealing: two cards to me. Two to him. I guess he knows we're not going to sleep any time soon, either. Everything is too wound up.

"Hold 'Em," Max says, a declaration, not a question. I think of Tommy Davis, who plays poker and has not been winning. But I breathe in, remembering how Max held me when I panicked, pulse tangling my veins.

"We don't have chips."

Max taps the side of my head gently. "Just imagine," he says.

We ante up our imaginary chips, two for him, two for me.

"So you know the game?"

I shrug. Of course I do.

Our cards lay between us on the bed, facedown.

"I'm dealer. You're the small blind," Max tells me. Blinds are bets you make before you see your cards. Before you know if you have any chance in hell.

We shove more imaginary chips into the imaginary pot.

Then we peek at our cards. He's dealt me a queen of clubs and a ten of diamonds.

"So here's my secret," Max says, even though I haven't asked him. He burns a card, then places three cards up on the white striped satiny comforter. A queen of spades, a jack of diamonds, a king of hearts.

Good for me. Maybe. I wait for him to impart his secret advice. *Size up your opponent. Don't bet more than you're willing to lose.*

But he says instead: "If you wait for premium cards, you'll be blinded off."

"So you bet with crap?"

"That's the trick."

"That's it?" He has not looked at his down cards since the first glance. His eyes have been on me.

We shove imaginary chips into the imaginary pot, raising our bets.

"Like I told you, Leo Leonora. It's not about being lucky. It's about making the other guy think you are."

He burns a second card. Deals the turn. Two of clubs.

We raise more bets with our imaginary chips.

Max's long fingers are agile as he burns the final card

and deals the river, the last common card. Queen of hearts.

Both of us can now claim the pair of queens.

"If you go all in against a more powerful player," Max says, and his face is absolutely serious, "it's one of two things. You face death or you weaken him."

He gestures to my cards, facedown still on the bed. "What say you, Leo Leonora?" He smiles and it's a real smile, warm and genuine, bright as the sun.

I push the rest of my imaginary chips into the invisible pile. "All in," I say.

"Call," says Max.

We show our cards.

Max has a seven of spades and an eight of diamonds.

My queen combines with the two queens for three of a kind.

"Gotcha!" I say, waving my arms in a seated victory dance.

I don't plan on kissing him, and I don't think he plans on kissing me. But he pulls me to him and our foreheads touch and then our lips and then he pulls me closer.

He tastes like fries and Coke and I think the pickles from the burgers. I am glad we had them hold the onions. His chin is scruffy because he hasn't shaved in a while, but I don't mind it. He cups my face with his hands. My heart beats like a tiny bird, flapping its wings inside me.

"Leo," Max says, his voice deep. His skin smells warm somehow. My breath dips like a roller coaster. "Leo," he repeats, voice rougher now. His mouth hovers near mine, not kissing again, but close.

Then he's pushing away, edging back fast like I'm dangerous or on fire. He blinks, twice, like he's surprised to see me.

"Leo," he says a third time. "I don't think . . . Shit. I shouldn't have . . . I mean, things are crazy. . . ."

He's off the bed now and pacing the room, and my heart is bumping for a million reasons including the one where I want him back against me.

"Your mother must wonder where you are," he says.

I shrug, not trusting my voice. I kissed him and now we're talking about my mother? God.

"You shouldn't be here with me, Leo," he says, sounding like a stranger. "I should take you home."

"What? Why?" I can still taste his lips on mine. "I—"

Max paces some more. "Do you really think your sister is in some kind of trouble? What was she mixed up with, anyway?"

"I, um. Yes. Maybe. I don't know. Nothing."

"But she took all your money."

"Well, yeah, but she wouldn't—"

"Of course she would. People do what they want, Leonora."

"Not Paris."

"Why not? Your sister is no different from anyone else. You either. Or me."

His words are like a slap. My brain freezes, trying to rec-
oncile this cold Max with the Max who came to get me, the
Max who tells physics jokes. The Max who just kissed me.

"People do all sorts of shit, Leo. They're not always
nice. Including me. And not just because I would lie to you
about liking frozen yogurt."

I'm standing now, too, even though I didn't notice that
I'd gotten up. Everything in me is running fast and then
faster. Would Paris have taken my money for herself? Why?

"It's not that much money, anyway," he says, and it's this
last one that stabs me hardest.

"Fuck you," I say because it seems the best—the only—
response at this moment. "I didn't force you to help me."

Tears sting my eyes and I turn my head so he won't see.

He sees anyway. I turn back and watch him register that
he's made me cry. He scowls.

"I didn't mean to—" he says.

"Yeah, you did."

"You . . . Leo . . . you." Max shoves his hand through
his hair hard. Then he does it again. He walks to the door.
"Stay here." The door thuds quietly behind him before I
can say another word.

THIRTEEN

I AM AN IDIOT. BECAUSE ONLY AN IDIOT TRUSTS A BOY SHE MEETS WHEN she brings him a piece of pie. A bigger idiot kisses him.

And then gets left in a hotel room.

My hands shake as I try Paris's cell again using Mom's phone. She doesn't answer. I call my own cell. She doesn't answer it either.

I try not to panic.

I fail.

"You can take a bus," I tell myself aloud. "Buses run to LA." Talking to myself just makes me feel more stupid. "You can take a cab home and steal the keys to your mother's car." Of course only if she's still asleep when I get there and not at work.

I shove my feet in my shoes.

Stay here, Max told me. Does that mean he's coming

back? Do I want him to come back? No.

What the hell have I been thinking?

I tell myself to sit down at the little table and think. Breathe. I am no worse off than I was, right?

Nope. I run out the door instead. It closes behind me before I realize I do not have a key card. Great. Now I am in the hallway of a hotel. Alone. With my stuff locked inside the room. My mother's phone, at least, is in my hand.

I am officially the stupidest girl in Las Vegas, and believe me, that is saying something.

Then from down the hall I hear, "You didn't take the extra key card, did you?"

Max Sullivan is striding toward me, long legs pistoning fast, boots slapping the carpet.

I don't know whether to smack him or laugh. Or maybe cry except I absolutely don't want to cry in front of him again. Because then he'll kiss me and then push me away and we already did that, right?

"You came back," I say.

"I said I was coming back."

"You said, 'Stay here.' Then you stormed out the door."

Max heaves a sigh. "Stormed is a bit strong. But . . . this isn't working, Leo."

This time the heat starts in my stomach and surges to my cheeks. He is infuriating. Only, looking at his expression, I guess I'm doing the same thing to him.

"I'll catch a cab," I say. "Just let me in for my stuff."

"What? No. I mean, you're not a girl who should be hanging out in a hotel room with me. Or anyone. I mean . . . Shit, Leo. I know what we planned. But you don't belong here."

"I said I'll get a cab."

He holds out his hand. "Not what I mean."

I duck out of reach. "Just let me in."

"Leo, I—"

"Let. Me. In."

He shoves his hand through his hair. Opens the door with his key card. Because of course he remembered to take one.

"Did you even get on the elevator?" I ask, pushing by him. "Inclinator. Whatever."

He laughs. "No."

"So this is funny?" I am so furious at him and all of this that I feel like I am going to explode. I grab my things, even the mushroom cloud T-shirt.

Max puts a hand on my arm. "Leo. I left my duffel bag in the room. I was obviously coming back. Calm down."

I yank my arm out of reach. "Don't touch me. And do not tell me to calm down."

He heaves another sigh. Looks up and down and then finally back at me. "I was going to the truck. To get the SAT prep book I have in there. But then I—"

"You . . . what?" My heart gives up rattling and just sits there. It seems as surprised as I am.

More hair shoving. More sighs. The scar over his brow waggles around and despite everything, it still does something quivery to my belly. What is wrong with me?

"C'mon. We're going," Max says, reaching for his duffel that's sitting by his bed. He does not unzip it to see if I've rifled through it in the approximately five minutes he was gone.

This time when he reaches for my hand, though, I let him lace his fingers with mine. His palm is warm and only the tiniest bit sweaty.

We walk together to the elevator. Ride on an angle down to the lobby.

"Do you think we should call it a downclinator now?" he asks, and even though I tell myself that I am planning on walking to the taxi line as soon as we get off this thing, I smile. Maybe there's nothing wrong with me. Maybe it's him.

What is the deal with you, Max Sullivan?

In the cavernous lobby, crowded and bustling, Max leads me across the vast marble floor, past palm trees and Egyptian statues, the floors above us angled inward, narrow swaths of light where rooms are. He is still holding my hand. I am still letting him.

"Sit," he says when we reach a black leather couch on the edge of one of the lounges.

I narrow my eyes. "I'm fine." I tug my hand from his. "Don't tell me what to do."

"Leo," Max says, his voice quiet yet somehow loud enough over the din of people and casino and music. "We're not ready to get on the road yet. But taking you up there was . . . Sit." He folds himself onto the couch slowly, like if he doesn't demonstrate I won't know what he means.

I keep standing.

"Let's say we had a lottery to select who got to stay in the most expensive room in this hotel for free. There are one hundred men, one hundred and fifty women, and two hundred couples whose names are placed in the hat. Each man's name is entered three times, each woman's name is entered two times, and each couples' name one time. What is the probability that a man's name will be chosen?"

I gape at him. But my brain is calculating because that's what my brain likes to do.

My mouth says, "Why are you doing this?"

Max says, "Because if I drive now, I'll fall asleep."

I frown. "Three-eighths," I say.

Max grins. "You're smart, Leo Leonora."

"I know. I'm going to Stanford."

"Life is about backup plans," Max says, looking at me and then away.

I am not smart about all things. But I don't need to hear it from him. Something close to anger swells, surprising me with its fierceness.

"Is Vegas your backup plan?"

He presses his lips together. This time his smile is as slanted as everything in this pyramid of a hotel. "I got into Rice. That was my first choice."

"And?"

He shrugs, eyes darker than they had been. "Deferred for the year."

"Well, good for you." I lower myself to the couch, balancing at the edge and then, after a few awkward seconds of glaring at him, scoot back. I know this signals that I'm staying. But plans can change.

"I like sliced tomatoes, too," he adds with no preliminary setup. "And chicken enchiladas and thin-crust pizza with mushrooms. Not together, obviously. And I didn't always live in Texas. I was born in upstate New York. We moved when I was seven. Also, I like country music. And don't make a face. It defines life. I have a whole set of theories. Also the original seasons of *Star Trek*. I bought the novelizations from some dude on eBay."

I raise an eyebrow. Who am I to judge someone's passions?

"I have a Captain Kirk impression," Max says.

"Everyone does that impression," I tell him. But he does his Kirk voice anyway, reading the next math problem like he's giving orders to the *Enterprise*.

I bite my lip so I won't laugh.

"It's a big hit at parties," he says.

"I'll bet."

He does the voice again. This time I laugh. I can't help it.

Which is how I end up studying for the SAT retake in the lobby of the Luxor Hotel while fake Egypt does its fake Egypt thing around us.

My sister has gone off to places unknown, probably LA. My heart stays jittery. Eventually I will find her even if it takes getting fired for missing work and driving across the desert to California.

I text her from Mom's phone while Max scribbles another equation on a cocktail napkin for me to solve, telling her that I'm coming to find her. To call me, please. Something. Anything. I dial her number and leave the same message on her voice mail.

No response.

Max hands me the sample problem. He's ordered us Cokes from the bar, and he slurps a sip of his. "This one is probably too easy for you," he says. "You're really good at probability, aren't you?"

I see the answer before I've even finished setting up the equation.

"You better come up with another one," I say, stubby keno pencil riding swiftly across the flimsy napkin, showing off, just a little.

He grins, squinting his eyes in a theatrical way to show me he's thinking.

"I'm not such a nice person either," I say. "Just so you know." I can tell he doesn't believe me—even with all his ranting about human nature—because he stops the theatrical squinting for a few seconds to roll his eyes.

Sometime after that, in the middle of another word problem, we lean our heads back and fall asleep. No one wakes us. Later I think we must look no odder than anything else in Las Vegas—two strangers studying SAT problems and drinking Cokes in the middle of the day while a few feet away, someone wins big at the poker tables.

It's the buzzing of Mom's phone that opens my eyes.

I blink, getting my bearings. Where the hell . . . Luxor. Bar. Math problems. Max—sleeping with his mouth slightly open on the couch next to me. My eyes feel gritty. What time is it?

I wrangle the phone from my pocket. The time glares up at me. Impossible. It is almost 10:00 p.m. Shit.

My sister has sent a text from my own missing phone to Mom's.

My insides contract.

Go to LA, Leo. I'm waiting for you. Where we were happy, Leo. You'll remember. Hurry.

FOURTEEN

I-15 FROM VEGAS TO LA IS A LONG LINE THROUGH THE DESERT, PUNCTU-
ated by a few towns here and there that maybe no one would
care about except that people stop there to stretch their legs.

We have changed clothes in the lobby bathrooms and
bought supplies (translate: junk food) for our road trip. I
have even brushed my teeth with a travel set Max got from
the concierge.

I am now wearing my *Have a Blast* T-shirt. From his
duffel bag, Max has switched into a faded pair of jeans that
hang low on his hips, a black T-shirt—fitted, not baggy—
and old but expensive-looking deck shoes. He looks good.
Very good. Even though I don't want to, I think of the feel
of his lips as they brushed briefly against mine. My heart
skitters.

We are really doing this. I am driving to Los Angeles

with Max Sullivan to find my sister.

"I can take you home still," Max says as we settle into his truck. His eyes look weary, but he holds my gaze.

"I know."

"Should I?" The question hangs between us, awkward as that air freshener tree.

Yes, I think. *Yes, you should. This is crazy. I am not a crazy person. I don't do things like this.*

Which is why she took my money. To make sure I'd go.

"No," I say. "Let's do this."

He hesitates, hand on the gearshift. Someone behind us honks loudly, a prolonged blare of sound.

"Leo," he begins. "I think maybe—"

"You want me to get out?" My voice is sharp. The night sky feels like it's forcing its way through the neon.

Max shoves the truck in gear. "California, here we come," he says. He flicks on the turn signal, and we join the line of traffic on Las Vegas Boulevard, the Luxor light shining into the sky behind us.

An hour out down the highway, sitting next to Max in the Ranger's small cab—two open cans of Monster in the cup holders between us—I am painfully aware that Max Sullivan has very specific preferences for road trip tunes.

"Gotta be country," he says as Garth Brooks sings about having friends in low places. "Or heavy metal. AC/DC is good traveling music. Metallica. And eighties rock ballads work. Eighties rock ballads got me from San Antonio to El Paso. But for long, lonely trips in the dark, nothing beats country."

"That is a well-defined opinion, Max."

Garth shifts to Carrie Underwood. I toss a handful of Apple Jacks—road trip snack of champions—into my mouth. A flimsy plastic sack of chips and jerky and bottled waters and Monsters rest at my feet. Also a six-pack of those tiny boxes of breakfast cereal—specifically the grossly sweet ones: the previously mentioned Apple Jacks (my favorite), Frosted Flakes, and Froot Loops. The ones you have to eat all of because otherwise they go stale as soon as they hit the air.

Carrie Underwood bellows about letting Jesus take the wheel.

"No offense," I say, crunching cereal. "But I don't get this song. I mean, it's not literal, right? Because you wouldn't be driving along, hit a patch of ice with your baby in the backseat, and then actually take your hands off the wheel, would you?"

"Jerky," Max says, and it takes me a few beats until I realize he wants me to hand him some, which I do.

"So it's a metaphor, then?" I rustle through the snack bag for a piece of jerky and work to unwrap it. We're passing through Primm now and this roadside casino called Buffalo Bill's. I can see the huge roller coaster that sits on the resort property.

Max snorts a laugh.

"Is it?" I hold the jerky out of reach, waiting for a better answer.

He snatches the strip from my hand. "You want Starbucks? There's one in Primm." He chomps a huge bite.

I look at him more carefully, with his one hand on the wheel, one feeding teriyaki-flavored soft beef jerky into his mouth. "You drive this a lot?"

Max finishes chewing. Swallows. "Now and then," he says, voice casual. "And yeah, it's a metaphor."

"But it's a country song. Aren't they like totally literal? I mean, I don't think people are listening to Carrie and thinking, Gee, this is a metaphor for her giving up control to a higher power. I think they're listening and thinking, Damn, she just took her hands off the wheel on black ice."

Max sighs. "So no to Starbucks?"

I toss back the remaining Apple Jacks. "How often do you go to LA?"

"Do you want me to change the music?"

I think about this. "No."

Carrie finishes giving Jesus directions and begins that one about taking a Louisville slugger to her cheating boyfriend's headlights and keying his four-wheel drive.

"Chick is into cars, huh?"

"Must be it."

"Do you believe that?" I slurp my Monster. Diet Monster tastes like shit, but it's more effective than coffee.

"Believe what?" Max looks at me, then back at the road. We're passing another casino complex, this one called Whiskey Pete's. "That Carrie Underwood likes vehicular songs?"

I swig more Monster, chemical aftertaste washing down the cereal's cloying sweetness. "Believe in giving up your problems to, well, whatever you believe in." I leave it vague because I'm not sure what *I* believe in. Or if I believe in anything.

Max's grip tightens on the wheel, which I take as a sign. "Leo," he says, "do you always ask this many questions on a road trip?"

"I don't go on many road trips." Then I blurt, "I haven't been much of anywhere really. Around California, mostly. Arizona once. Here."

"That's it?" Max says, and I feel myself blush. He looks at me briefly, narrowing his eyes, then sliding his gaze to the road. "I mean, here is okay, too," he adds quickly.

I don't think he means it. I suspect Max has been more places than just Texas and upstate New York. Right now we are not anywhere. Just traveling west.

I could tell him all the trips I have planned in my head. A long list of places I would like to go and the things I will do when I get there. New York City and Paris, London and Rome. Italy in general, where I will eat pizza and gelato, and this place called the Amalfi Coast and then on to Spain and maybe even Portugal. I will wander the great museums and meet people and maybe I will even study abroad for a semester if I can figure out a way to afford it. Scotland maybe. Or Ireland. Stanford has a program where you can study at Trinity College in Dublin. I look at the pictures online and imagine myself walking the cobblestones and sitting in the pubs. I tell myself that one day I will really go.

It is not only Paris who dreams of getting out of the desert.

I want to go as far as I can. This is what I promise myself. I want more—much more—than hurtling through the night toward something over which I have no control.

Max doesn't answer the part about what he believes, and after a few more miles, I let it drop. What do I want him to say? *Yes, Leo, I think we should give up our problems to our personal higher power of choice and everything will get solved and saved and wrapped all neat and tidy with a pretty pink bow?*

We drive through the night, traffic surprisingly steady on both sides, mountains deep shadows in the distance. Who are all these people, coming and going between Vegas and LA? Are they searching for someone, too?

My insides constrict as I think about Paris. Why did she disappear last night and not the night before or the night before that? Why leave me these notes and messages in some strange scavenger hunt? Why LA?

What's underneath it all, at the core?

Maybe nothing.

A piece of paper is a piece of paper. Taking your hands off the wheel is taking your hands off the wheel. A physical motion. A movement through time and space. Nothing more.

Maybe Max won't answer my question because there is no answer. He works at the Atomic Testing Museum, not Yogiberry. Every day he shows people that movie with the mushroom cloud. People blow each other up. People unleash crap that can't ever be taken back.

What else is there to know?

We pass the sign for Zzyzx Road. I think there are hot springs down there somewhere if you get off. Mostly I think someone named it so it would be famous. The road at the end of the alphabet or whatever.

Max and I both make snoring sounds, mimicking the letters. We do this loudly so we can hear each other over Kenny Chesney wondering why he and a girl are not in love. I-15 is skirting the Mojave Desert now, a whole lot of empty punctuated by not very much. If we drove off the highway, we could lose ourselves in it.

"I like the desert," Max says abruptly as Kenny Chesney melds into the Band Perry, singing about not wanting to be lonely. "All that space."

I think about this as the truck bumps along, darkness pressing on each side of us.

"I guess everyone's something," I say. "Ocean. Mountain. Desert."

"You're ocean, right?"

"Definitely ocean."

"Deep," Max says, joking. But I think it's true. The ocean hides stuff down deep where no one can see.

About ninety miles out, I have to pee.

"Baker's not far," Max says. He agrees it would be nice to stretch his legs.

Two things are notable just off the highway in Baker: Bob's Big Boy, with the statue of Big Boy himself holding that double-decker burger in his palm. And the World's Largest Thermometer.

I have no idea why someone decided to build a big-ass thermometer here in Baker, except maybe because it's the last stop before you turn off into Death Valley. So maybe being hot was on people's minds.

But right now, it's cold here, and there's a wind rising off the Mojave. I shiver when I step from the truck and Max reaches behind him and fishes out a gray hoodie from where he's tossed the duffel and the books and the rest of his traveling life.

"Thanks," I say, slipping it on. The inside is pilled from wear, but it's soft and warm. It smells both slightly musty and slightly like Max. I hug it to me as the wind whips around us.

In Bob's Big Boy, Max orders two coffees to go. We use the bathrooms. The tired-looking waitress who hands us our coffees—for which I insist on paying—reminds me of

Maureen at the Heartbreak.

Then we walk outside, sipping our coffees and staring up at the huge thermometer across the street.

"Impressive," Max says.

"It's big," I agree. "Weird, though, right? Someone thinking this up. Like someone had to decide, you know? I am going to build an enormous thermometer RIGHT HERE."

"It's physics," Max says, and I snort a quick laugh. But he adds, "Newton's first law of motion, remember? We make shit up until something stops us. That's the way it works." He waggles a brow like he's kidding, but his voice is serious.

"Every object in a state of uniform motion tends to remain in that state of motion unless an external force is applied to it," I say, going with it. He's right, though. We move from place to place and build giant thermometers and fake pyramids and fake Eiffel Towers and casinos big enough to get lost in because that's what we do.

"Exactly." He tilts his head back, eyes to the sky.

Together, we stare some more at this freak of human construction. It makes as much sense for it to be here as anything else that's been going on. I think that's why I like science. Because science works to make sense of things. Science is not your sister leaving cryptic clues that make your heart pound but don't add up.

"Maybe some architect was running away," I say, not

even thinking about how it sounds until it's out of my mouth. "And he got to Baker and decided this was the place to make his mark."

Max looks at me then, something sad and wistful crossing his face. Above us, the stars glitter like hard little diamonds.

"Doesn't change things," he says. "The running away."

I hesitate.

"I don't know," I tell him eventually, and it feels like the truth. "Probably not."

Above us, some nocturnal bird swoops through the inky sky, dipping low and then lower, skimming over the desert until I lose sight of it in the dark. The vastness feels both dangerous and comforting, so huge after the truck's small, cramped space.

"Paris gets on these binges sometimes," I say. "Since we were kids. Especially when things felt . . . not good. When Mom would move us to this place or that. Paris would get out her art pencils and draw picture after picture. They were like the stories I used to tell her. Two sisters living in a castle. With servants. And a moat. And some big dog with a slobbery tongue. Also a handsome prince for each of them. The one for the girl I knew was supposed to be me had blue spiky hair, a pointy chin, and anime bangs. In case you were wondering." I manage a small smile. "It felt like—I don't know. Like she could make it better somehow."

Max scrapes a thumb over his chin. Somewhere in the

night, something howls, a thin, high-pitched sound. "You can't always fix things."

We're both quiet then, and I think about Paris and me and how we used to wander Santa Monica. Spend afternoons at that old movie theater, sitting together in the dark, laughing and watching stories spin out on the screen.

"Watch out for each other," Mom told us, as though in saying this, it got her off the hook. But she was looking at me when she said it, and I think what she really meant was more one-sided. That I had to watch out for Paris. That this is how it was for us.

"You have to understand my mother," I say to Max, surprised I break the silence first. Surprised I'm telling him. "She's smart, but she likes someone to take care of her."

"Doesn't everyone?"

I wait until I assess that he is serious. "You know how she met Tommy? In a restaurant parking lot in LA. Our car had a flat. She thought he was cute, so she asked him if he knew how to change a flat tire."

"That's bad?"

"She was the top salesperson at Harley Davidson. My mother can change a tire blindfolded."

"Oh," says Max.

A few feet away, another couple—a real couple, I think, not just two people thrown together by pie and a missing sister—embrace. The guy is tall and slender, thinner than Max, and even though it's freezing out here, the girl is wearing a short summery dress and cowboy boots. They're hugging and she's pressed against him tight, her hands in his jeans pockets. They kiss then, a long kiss that lasts and lasts and I think of how Max kissed me at the Luxor, but I know it's not the same.

"Good for them," I say, voice coming out brittle. I clear my throat.

"Maybe they just met each other," Max says, eyes laughing now—maybe about the blue-haired prince my sister had imagined for me—but there's something sadder in them, too, just for a second. "They were eating cheeseburgers at the Big Boy and he put mustard on his fries and that was that. Well, after they ate some pie." He grins.

I shake my head. "She's on a diet. No pie for her."

Max nods. "You are right, Leo Leonora. How could I have missed that?"

"I'm smart, remember?" I tap a finger to my forehead.

But when they kiss again, Max says, "We need to go," and he's no longer smiling.

"They'll probably break up tomorrow," I say, trying to lighten the mood.

He doesn't react.

"Maybe then she'll eat the pie," I say, even though it sounds sexist. I wait for Max to say something clever and quippy and ironic. But he doesn't.

"You break up with someone lately?" I ask, because it's suddenly obvious that maybe he has.

Max circles his tongue around the inside of his cheek. "Yeah."

A million thoughts ramble through my brain. Who was she? Is she the real reason he's on the run?

"It happens," I say lamely.

"Oh?" He barely glances at me.

My skin heats. "Well, not to me. I mean, I . . . I haven't gone with anyone long enough to break up with them." And now he knows it.

I am grateful when he doesn't respond. And possibly grateful there is no girl back in Texas waiting for him.

We walk to the truck and climb inside. It still smells musty and stale, but familiar, too, and I buckle my seat belt, settling in. Max shoves the gearshift into drive. We bounce over gravel to the entrance ramp, then out to the highway. The sky is filled with stars. In Vegas there's so much neon I barely remember the sky is there.

I sneak a look at Max. When this is over, will I see him again? Is he someone I *want* to see? The way my heart lunges both surprises me and lets me know the answer. Yes.

Is it yes for him, too?

In my pocket, Mom's cell vibrates sharply.

Another text from Paris. From my phone.

I need you to do this, Leo. You'll figure it out once you're in LA.

My hands go slick around the phone. Outside the truck, the wind spirals a cold blast that sneaks in with us. I shiver under the sleeves of Max's loaner hoodie.

"What if I don't find her?" The words come louder than I want.

Max's eyes linger on me briefly, then he turns his attention back to the road. "Leo, I . . . you're sure Paris wants to be found?"

The question makes my heart lurch.

"Of course she does," I snap.

He presses his lips together.

"I'm sorry," I say. "I didn't mean to . . . I mean, I really appreciate that you're—"

Max reaches out his hand, rests it briefly on my knee. I freeze, then realize he's being nice.

"We all have our secrets," he says. "Maybe she . . ." He trails off.

I bite my lip. What is he really asking? My heart is a trip-hammer now and I don't want it to be.

I pat his hand awkwardly, and he puts it back on the wheel. "She'd never hurt me. We take care of each other, Paris and me."

Max clears his throat. "Maybe you more than her?"

"No," I say, but I think he doesn't agree.

We drive more miles and Max plays more country medley, and what do you know, it's Taylor Swift. If anyone can sing about love gone wrong, it's Taylor. "I thought I had you figured out," she croons. "Something's gone terribly wrong."

"Why do you want to be a doctor?" Max asks abruptly, totally confusing me.

I tell him the same things I'd told my school counselor: I'm good with science and math. That it would be like solving puzzles every day. That I could make sick people better, take broken people and put them back together.

He looks straight ahead as I talk. Now and then, he nods his head so I know he's listening. "It's a lot of school," he says when I'm done.

True.

Also, not the reaction I usually get. When I tell people I am going to be a doctor, they nod approvingly. You are smart. You are special. You are driven.

If I told them the truth, that the *idea* of being a doctor—walking around in a lab coat, listening to people's chests with a stethoscope, scribbling out a prescription on one of those little white pads—is more real to me than any clear sense of what it will be like to actually do the job, those looks would fade. I know this as sure as I know anything.

I do not tell them I am just a girl who lives in a too-small house in a place I never wanted to be.

We hit a bump in the road, and my gaze snaps from the window. Max glances over, his face lit orange by the dash.

"What if you had a patient you couldn't help?"

"Why?" I try to read his face, but he looks back at the

road, hands on the wheel, giving me nothing.

"What if things went wrong? What if you weren't as good as you thought?"

His words make me flinch. My heart scrapes at my ribs. Does he think I can't do it?

"I guess you learn to deal with it," I say, hoping this sounds doctorly. "I mean, you do the best you can, I guess. Not everybody gets better. Or not better enough."

It is a weak answer and I know it. But what does he expect me to say?

He's quiet again, just more country music—someone I don't know—and the thump of the tires rolling over the road. But he shoots another glance at me, hard enough that my heart gives a thump with the tires. Max Sullivan does not know me well enough to question my career plans.

"What about you?" I ask, knowing I sound snippy again, but his question has made me edgy. "Why do you want to research or be an engineer or whatever?" He's been pretty vague about the whole thing.

Silence.

We bump along in the dark, squinting now and then in the light from oncoming traffic.

"You'll go to Rice, right?" I say, to fill the quiet between us. "After this year off. I mean, you'll have all the money you earned, which is great. I guess it's smart to take, what do they call it? A gap year. And research. What's biophysics, anyway? Is it really a combination of the two or—"

Max reaches over and yanks his iPod cord out of the dash—a sudden, violent sort of motion. I stop rambling. His eyes stay fixed on the road. My pulse jolts hard.

"You ever fail at something big, Leo Leonora?"

What?

"Does losing my sister count?"

He doesn't laugh, not even a chuckle.

"I have," says Max Sullivan.

Thoughts of the "charge it to the Sullivans" store and all the rest of what he's told me fly through my brain. None of it seems enough to run from. If I told him all my truths, what kind of silence would there be in this truck then?

He sighs audibly, and I find myself irritated.

I say, "You didn't make valedictorian? You didn't ace your SATs?"

More silence. I watch the numbers tick on the odometer. We hurtle along through the night.

It occurs to me that I am driving in the desert with a stranger.

"There was a girl," Max says, not looking at me. My heart skips a beat. "Her name is Ashley. She's why I left."

There is something so stark about the way he says it that tears sting the backs of my eyes. Did he get her pregnant? My heart slides into my throat.

"Max," I say, eyes on him even though he won't look at me. "You don't have to tell me."

"If I do, will you listen?"

I hesitate, watching him watch the road.

"Yes," I say.

He says, "You may not like what you hear."

"I'm tough," I say, trying for lightness, but he still won't look at me.

A semi whizzes by us, and the truck sways hard. Max pulls the wheel, swears under his breath.

"Everyone's damaged, Max," I say quietly. "One way or another. Even those annoying people who always look happy."

The truck has stopped shaking but not my hands and I tuck them under my legs to still them. What if I just told Max everything right now? But I can't. I won't.

"Okay," Max says.

"I grew up on Tennyson Street. A neighborhood called West University. Big brick house, nice lawn, pool. The whole thing. My mom teaches yoga. My dad's a professor at Rice. Physics."

"Well, that explains the geek jokes."

Max gives me the smallest of smiles. Another mile ticks by.

"I'm the youngest—you know, the oops kid. My sister's ten years older, my brother's in the middle. They both work in DC now. He teaches school. She's a doctor. But my parents had money by the time I was born. We took a lot of vacations. Skiing in Aspen. A lake house in Austin. That kind of thing."

I nod my head like I'm familiar with "that kind of

thing." I have skied once, up in Big Bear. But it was a long time ago and I know it is *not* the same thing. Except for the going-down-the-mountain part.

Max goes on about playing soccer and football and doing well in his classes.

"I was valedictorian at Lamar," he says. "You were wrong about that."

I shoot him a brief glance, but he's looking straight ahead.

"So Ashley," I say gently as a truck rushes past us in the dark.

"Ashley was my girlfriend. We started going out the end of junior year. Ashley Pennington. Ashley Maude Pennington, actually, although she'd probably be pissed that I told you her middle name. Tall. Blond. Soccer team. Smart. Real smart. Me—I have to study. But Ash—it was easy for her. Pretty much everything."

"But you were number one," I say.

"Well," says Max, and is quiet again. The pine tree air freshener and his museum tag sway in the endless rush of AC.

I try to picture what Ashley Maude Pennington would look like: Tall and willowy—the kind of girl who picks just the right little black dress that shows off her tan bare legs with well-muscled calves. She gets sweaty playing soccer and she's got toned arms with only the faintest of little blond hairs on smooth skin and solid abs. She never smells like chemical frozen yogurt because her family has buckets of money and she doesn't have to work at Yogiberry unless she wants to.

"We were that couple," Max says. "That 'walk through the hall arms around each other' couple. The couple that everyone wants to be—athletic, accepted to good colleges, in all the right classes."

"Did you love her?" The question flees my mouth before my brain knows what I want him to answer.

"No." He lets the word hang, dangling at eye level like the ugly air freshener.

"I thought I did," Max says then. "She was, well, we . . ." He frowns but doesn't turn his head. "She wasn't the one. I knew it—had known it even before that. But it was April. Two weeks before prom. She'd planned it all for us. The group we were going with. The limo. The restaurant. The beach house in Galveston we'd all rented for after. I was going to drive down the afternoon before prom and drop off the booze and the food. It was all set. The dress. My tux. The flowers."

His hands are tight on the wheel. He is still looking absolutely straight ahead—like a sea captain searching for a whale or an iceberg, maybe.

"There was this party at UT. Ash wanted to do the sorority thing. She was a legacy through her mom. Kappa. That's one of the big ones. She went with a couple of her friends."

My heart is thudding again because whatever's coming, it's not good.

"So the thing is, Leo Leonora. I was going to break up with her. After prom. I knew I was. I knew we'd be *that* couple, too. The ones who do it on the beach after prom with a bottle of champagne making it classy and then the next morning one of them picks a fight—publicly so there's no going back. And everyone is still hungover when the rumors start burning up their cell phones and by the time we all get home, it's over."

"Max," I say, but I don't think he even hears me.

"She went to a frat party that weekend. At UT. She got very, very drunk." He takes a drink of his long-gone-cold coffee. Swallows audibly. Then sips more.

"She was very drunk, Leo." His voice sounds far away.

"So she cheated on you?"

"No. I don't know. Maybe."

Something worse than cheating? How much worse?

"The frat house had a balcony on the second floor. That's where she fell. She'd been drinking—her blood alcohol level was off the charts. She tumbled over the balcony and slammed into the concrete."

I wait for him to tell me she's dead. That this is what he's running from—the dead girl he was going to break up with. I hold my breath.

"Permanent brain damage. A dent in her head. The vision in her left eye shot to shit. Motor function impaired. Speech slurred. You get the picture."

I put my hand on his arm, but he shakes it off. My brain

fills with the image of beautiful, damaged Ashley. In this version, she has a thin, twisted blue-and-yellow thread bracelet around her tanned wrist.

"You know what I really think about science, Leo? About all those theories and talk of black holes and dark matter? They're just theories. All that logic? It's just crap."

"It's not crap." My voice sounds thin. "It's not," I repeat, stronger this time. "The theory of relativity? The elements? Cures for diseases? They're real, Max. You know that. You work at a science museum. You explain things to kids."

He makes a noise in the back of his throat. "You know what the world did with Einstein's theory? They made weapons of mass destruction."

I glare at him. "But that doesn't make it crap."

"You know why Alfred Nobel founded the Peace Prize? Because he invented dynamite. He was trying to make amends."

"Are you saying Einstein was sorry about figuring out the theory of relativity? Because I don't think—"

"I'm saying that people do horrible things and sometimes there's no making it better." The pain in his voice swells around us.

My stomach knots hard and I press my clasped hands against it.

"You don't know me," I say after a few beats. "You don't have to say the rest of it."

For many more miles he doesn't. We just drive, and LA

gets closer and closer, and I think about Ashley, this damaged girl who he never loved. I have no right to the rest of
the story. It's not like he owes me any truths.

But the silence grows louder and even though we're in the
middle of nowhere—not anyone's favorite place to be—I
say, "Pull over." And when he glances at me confused, forehead wrinkling, I say it again. "There," I tell him, pointing
to an exit with a sign for an In-N-Out Burger. I'm not even
sure where we are, exactly. I haven't been looking.

I don't want to stop. I don't even know why we've gone
this far in the first place except that it has happened and
we're here and my sister is still missing.

Max doesn't say anything then, just pulls off the highway and comes to a stop on the side of the access road.
Way in the distance I can see the red-and-yellow In-N-Out
sign glowing. The truck feels too small—even more than
it has—and so I open the door and climb, waiting for him
to follow, a part of me tense until I'm sure he's not going to
just peel away and leave me here.

We lean against the truck as it settles and ticks and the
heat from the engine sifts into the air. The sky is still inky
and studded with stars.

My own truths flicker over my tongue, waiting. But I
am not brave, not really. Not yet. Maybe not ever.

"Here's what I know about black holes," I say, looking at
the sky. "They happen when huge stars die and collapse on
themselves. But when a star goes supernova, the particles

explode everywhere. That's what I read. So if you think about it, we're all made of stardust, see? Tiny particles that filtered into everything."

I don't look at him, but I can feel Max's shoulders seem to relax a bit.

"That's all I've got," I tell him. Because honestly, it is. I don't know that much about the stars.

Max snorts, a rather rude-sounding noise.

"You are not a great comfort, Leo Hollings."

"Never said I was." But I'm smiling inside at the oddly soothing sound of his voice. I realize that over the past hours I've grown used to listening to him talk.

Over on the highway, traffic whooshes by. We stay leaning against the truck, our shoulders touching lightly. His fingertips brush mine briefly, but he does not take my hand and I do not offer it.

"What you have to understand, Leo Leonora, is that I'm the guy who always does the right thing. That's just who I am." He holds up three fingers in the Boy Scout salute.

"And they all expected me to—I don't know what they expected. That I would be at the hospital with her. Of course. That I would sing to her and talk to her and visit her every day and bring her flowers and teddy bears and act like she was exactly the same."

His fists clench and he breathes in through his nose, holding it a long time before he exhales. Behind us, someone honks a car horn, a short staccato blast. Max keeps his eyes on an invisible horizon.

"Not just her parents and mine. But everybody. Our friends. The teachers at school. Our coaches. I was going to break up with her, Leo. And now there she was in that damn hospital bed looking at me like I was the only thing she had left. You know what her mom said to me? 'She'll be okay as long as you're here.' Like if I wasn't, she wouldn't make it."

Max glances at me now, just for a second. "Her friend Courtney came to me. She was crying. And she said that Ash had cheated on me with some frat guy while she was drunk. But shit. What was I supposed to do with that? Take it as an excuse not to visit? Why would she tell me that, anyway? Hell, I didn't even know if it was true."

I try to find the words to help him. But I don't know what they are. So I say his name, "Max." And then: "Oh Max." Which is about as lame of a comfort as you can get.

"I ran anyway," Max says, and by then of course I know that's what has happened. "Deferred my acceptance to Rice—which about killed my father. My mother, too. Ever see a yoga teacher lose it? Well, neither had I. You want to know how I got this scar over my eyebrow? Prom. Me and a bottle of Jim Beam. In my room. Pathetic, right? Drunk on your own bed on prom night instead of going to sit with your brain-damaged girlfriend like a good boy. Slammed the glass down on the floor and it breaks and this piece flies up and cuts me. More pathetic. I didn't even know it happened until the blood started trickling into my eye. My father stormed in and starts screaming at me to 'Do the right thing. Stop being so self-absorbed.' You know what's worse? I thought about walking out while he was shouting, but you know why I didn't? Because I was too afraid that I'd stumble into the street and get hit by a car as some kind of karmic punishment."

He doesn't pull back when I squeeze his hand. His palm rests warm against mine. After a few beats, I let go.

"I couldn't do it, Leo. If I did it then, I'd be doing it forever. Forever's a long damn time."

I want to tell him that he is not horrible. That maybe I understand now why he has chosen to drive with me through the desert to find someone who means nothing to him. But in this moment, leaning so close to each other, it is easier to be silent.

After a while, we get back in the truck.

The last of the miles roll and we drive without talking, and at some point I ask him if he wants to put Taylor Swift back on and he does. And then we're in Hesperia and Victorville and then San Dimas and past the split from the 15 to the 515 that could take us to Pomona. Once when I whined that something wasn't fair, my sister told me, "If you want fair, go to Pomona." Because that's where the California State Fair was.

Remembering it now, I find myself laughing and tell Max why, and then he's laughing, too, a quiet, hesitant laugh. I think he is waiting for me to judge him for his choices. To tell him he's a lost cause for leaving Ashley, for running. That he has done something unforgivable. I can feel it pulsing from

him, surrounding us in the truck that has been our world
for hours now. But judging Max is not something I can do.
So we laugh together at my sister's joke that isn't funny. And
I think again what I've thought on and off for hours: that
somehow Paris has figured out a way to stick with me even as
she's disappeared.

It's heading toward five in the morning when we finally
roll into LA, I-10 strangely empty because it's too early for
the traffic.

I call Paris—again—on Mom's phone. "I'm in LA," I say
when it skips immediately to voice mail. "I'm here. Call me.
Text me. Something." I don't hang up right away, then realize
I'm idiotically waiting for her voice to pop out of thin air, like
a magician's trick.

It doesn't. She doesn't call. Or text. Or anything.

I do not admit to Max that some tiny part of me had still
expected Paris to call back. Or that I am panicked again in a
million ways for a million secret reasons.

"Where to?" Max asks. He sounds bone weary.

I don't know what to tell him. LA's a big city. But maybe—
more than maybe—there is only one place that makes sense.

Not long after that, Max Sullivan and I are standing in
front of the white statue of my mother's favorite saint, the sun
barely thinking about rising behind us.

"Hey, Monica," I say.

FIFTEEN

THE BEACH AT SANTA MONICA IS LONG AND VERY WIDE. LOTS OF DIS-
tance between the start of the sand and the start of the
ocean. But I like walking at the water's edge, so that's where
we go.

We have seen Monica and I've tapped her feet for luck.
It is too early to do anything else.

"So your mother really believed Saint Monica listened
to her?" We've kicked off our shoes, carrying them now as
we walk. The packed sand is cold and hard under my feet,
and I'm glad for Max's hoodie. The Pacific Ocean stretches
out to our right as we meander toward the pier, the rush of
waves filling my ears and chest, spray from the surf dotting
my arms.

"I don't know if it mattered," I say once I've thought it
over. "I think it was enough that she could say hello."

Max threads his long fingers with mine. Our thumbs wrap around each other. I try not to think about how good it feels. Because this—whatever this is—can't possibly last.

"Do you talk to her?" I ask, not sure I want to know. "Ashley, I mean."

Max shakes his head.

We walk some more at the water's edge, sand bunching cold and grainy under our toes. I think about slipping my hand away and putting it in his back pocket, but I don't. Our hips bump lightly as we watch the waves roll in and out, leaving white froth in their wake. I dip my toes in the freezing Pacific. The surf splashes my ankles.

Max lets go of my hand and spreads his arms wide, facing the ocean. A long wingspan of Max Sullivan. "It smells primal, doesn't it? Like it's got everything that's ever been."

"Including crap that keeps washing up from that tsunami in Japan," I say, because we've had enough deep thinking for like twelve lifetimes. But I tell him I'm impressed with the *primal*. "Ten-dollar word," I say.

Max scrunches his nose at me. His eyes are laughing.

In my pocket where I've shoved it, Mom's cell vibrates against my thigh. Paris. My hopes rocket.

But my stomach sinks as I read the text: *Get your ass home and stop worrying your mother. And tell your sister to get home, too.*

Tommy.

This stolen phone has been my thin but hopeful tether

to Paris, but now I heave it into the water. When it washes back up in the surf, I grab it again, breathing hard, nails digging into the wet sand, then wade into the water, the cold biting at my ankles and calves. I hurl the phone once more into the dark ocean—as far as I can.

This time it disappears.

It's not like it was helping me find her, was it?

Max looks like he wants to say something when I slosh back to him, but he doesn't. Just pulls me into a hug and we stand like that for a while, my legs dripping, then drying.

The sky is big above us and the Pacific stretches out and out, far away to places I've never been. Max's arms holding me, his skin warm against mine.

Something inside me shifts, a little and then more. I wrap my arms around Max's neck. Pull him close, then closer. Or maybe it's both of us, leaning in.

"Leo," Max says, his lips against my hair and the deep, even sound of his voice makes my belly contract over and over, swamping me with feeling: his skin, his mouth, the solidness of his body pressing against mine.

No one has ever held me like this. No one has ever made me feel that no matter what, maybe, just maybe, everything will work out.

I take it all in, telling myself to remember. To savor each molecule that's connecting us. The sun. The sky. Max's arms around my waist. The way his palm brushes against my cheek and his fingertip traces, gentle as a breeze, over my eyelids.

This time when our lips meet, it feels mutual, the best kind of kiss. Max's tongue slides against mine, salty and warm. His hands grip my hips. Boy smell fills my nose, and the kiss deepens, sending tingles down my body, making me dizzy with sensation. I slip my hands under his shirt, press them to his smooth, bare skin. He makes a low sound and pulls me closer, fingers massaging the nape of my neck, kissing the corner of my mouth and then all of it, a rush of lips and breath and tingles.

It is the kiss I've wanted my entire life. The kiss I thought existed only in movies or books.

Overhead, a seagull gives a sharp cry. The air smells like ocean and sky and Max.

We sink to the sand, still kissing, still pressed against each other. I am happy and scared and a million other feelings. He is muscle and smooth skin and rough jaw and sweet breath. He kisses my eyelids. I kiss the tip of his straight, pretty nose. His lips move back to mine and mine to his. Quick, eager kisses.

"Leo," Max says over and over, "Leo." His voice forms my name, the sound echoing in my head like a mediation. A prayer. It is perfect and beautiful and I think if nothing else good ever happens in my life, this moment might be enough.

Max strokes a hand through my hair, and for the first time in a while I stop believing the purple streak in my bangs was a mistake. He nuzzles kisses on my neck—each one sending me flying. I run my index finger over his scar, that tiny white line above his eyebrow. He wraps his hand around mine as I lift it away, kisses my fingertips.

No one has kissed me like this. Certainly not Buddy Lathrop. Not anyone. I have not kissed anyone back like this. It feels somehow both wonderful and dangerous and I cannot get enough of it.

Then Max leans back to look at me. "I like seeing you smile," he says. "I like seeing you happy."

Happy. My brain, so busy with kissing, engages. *Leo,* it says. *This is not why you've driven all the way to LA.*

But it is hard—no, impossible—to let go of this moment, this kiss. This everything.

Max brushes his lips against mine again, light as a feather, setting my nerve endings on fire. I tell my brain to shut up. We collapse together gently onto the sand and he covers me with his body, our legs entwined and everything pulsing with sensation.

LeoandMax, I think as we kiss, our names combining into one sound.

"Hey look," says a girl's voice from somewhere that is not here, underneath Max, who is currently kissing the sensitive hollow of my neck.

"What?" says another girl's voice as Max shifts to press a trail of tiny kisses up my jaw and onto the tender spot just under my ear, and my already tingling skin is now aching with the need for him to keep doing that.

"Tide washed up someone's cell," says the original voice.

I push Max off me and sit up, shaking sand from my hair. Two early-morning joggers—shorts, sports bras, Nikes, blond hair pulled back—stare down at what is probably my mother's cell phone that the tide has washed in yet again and is now sucking back out to sea.

Max reaches for me, but I pull away again, and eventually he turns and sees what I see.

"I am not going to take this as a sign," I tell him. "I really am not."

He smiles his crooked smile, eyes a mixture of amused and sad. Breathes in and out, then claps his hands together. "So where to now?"

Good question. We were happy here in LA, in Santa Monica, at least happier. But where is Paris?

"Somewhere you both liked, maybe?" Max suggests. My gaze is on his mouth, on that slightly fuller lower lip, and what I really want is to kiss him some more. "Wouldn't that make sense?"

"We don't like the same things," I say, because it's true.

Max pushes up in one fluid motion. He holds out a hand to me, but I rise on my own, brushing sand off my clothes.

"There has to be something," he says. "Some place you went. Some things you did." He smiles—the full-on type of Max smile now, bright as the sun that's shining over our heads. "Like I don't know. Bowling? Karaoke? Bingo? Square-dancing?"

I make a face. Despite the smile, his tone sounds arti-ficial, like he's trying too hard, and this sends up a brief warning signal, which I choose to ignore.

"You went places with her, though, right?"

Maybe it's the ridiculous image of Paris and me square-dancing—something neither of us would do *ever*. Maybe it's being back here in Santa Monica, the familiar smells and sights and sounds washing over me, seeping into my pores. The scent of salt water. The crisp blue of the California sky. The quirky shops lining the streets that lead to the beach. Air that isn't dry and endlessly heated and people doing things other than racing to yet another air-conditioned, sealed-up casino.

Maybe it's none of those. But suddenly, I know, the answer rising in my brain effortlessly, connecting me to my sister in a way that no washed-up cell phone could ever do.

Not just where Paris was happy. But where Paris and I were happy. The two of us.

I'm laughing then, because it's so obvious. Of course. Of course. Of course. In my head, I see the two of us, paying our admission with nickels and dimes from that ridiculous plastic sack of change.

"The movies," I say. "Beach Cinema. God, Max. How could I not—it won't be open until like noon. But that's it. It has to be. We spent a lot of afternoons there. I bet that's where she is."

"You sure?" Max does not look convinced. He hands

me his phone. "Tell her that's where we're headed. If you're right, then she'll know you figured it out and she'll be watching for you."

I debate this with him for a minute. I don't want to spook her somehow or make her come up with another note and send me on another wild goose chase. Max argues that she needs to know we're on our way.

"I guess," I say.

I text her that we'll meet her at Beach Cinema when it opens. *Up at the bar*, I type. *Like we used to.*

Then I explain to Max as we walk across the beach and up to the street. *It's over*, I think. *This whole thing is finally over.*

I do not assess if this is good or bad.

Beach Cinema, I tell Max, is this tiny theater off the Promenade, not too far from the little apartment we'd been subletting. It's old—built in the twenties—and has one of those huge marquees out front and a second-floor balcony and in the upstairs lobby there's a bar. A real, functioning bar with a bartender and a small variety of drinks and snacks, too, and little round tables and rickety old mismatched chairs and a sofa that looks like it came from Goodwill or someone's garage.

"The bartender was almost always this guy Oscar," I tell Max as we pass Saint Monica again and reflexively I trace my fingers across her feet but don't stop walking.

"We were underage for the booze, obviously," I say as we head up Wilshire, palm trees lining the streets like tropical soldiers, leaving Monica to guard the beach without us. The old record shop I remember is still there, and this Mexican restaurant, and the pretty boutiques with clothes I can't afford. I glance briefly at a leather bomber jacket on the mannequin in one window.

"But Oscar liked us. He was one of those guys where it's hard to tell how old he is. Fifty maybe? Maybe he was sixty. He had this long ponytail and he wore mostly tie-dyed shirts and cargo shorts and he had a tattoo of a bird on the side of his neck. I think he'd been working there since before we were born or something. He'd always give us Cokes, me and Paris. He'd pour them in real glasses and then he'd take one of those plastic sword toothpick things that you put in cocktails and he'd stab up a bunch of maraschino cherries—four or five for each of us all jammed on the plastic sword—and put those in our glasses. We used to joke that maybe he liked me better than Paris because sometimes he'd hand me a shot glass full of extra cherries."

The sun is shining and it's morning in LA, the breeze blowing off the Pacific and the air warming but cool. Sand is still sifting off our clothes and my lips are having this perfect skin memory of Max's delicate, shivery kisses.

I think about Beach Cinema as Max and I step into our shoes and he waits while I bend to lace up my Converse. Sometimes they would have movie marathons and Paris and I would stay there all day. They'd start at ten and by the time we left at four or five, we'd be full of popcorn and fizzy drinks, our lips sticky from all those cherries, our brains swirling with happy endings.

Then another memory rises unbidden. The first time Tommy Davis stayed over at our apartment back in LA, I woke up and there he was drinking coffee at our kitchen table and then there we were, talking about movies and how he liked those old black-and-white ones. Mom wasn't a movie person—not like Tommy was. Grammy Marie either. I had never talked to an adult who liked something I did.

Later I realized that he was just showing off. He'd heard me and Paris talking about this marathon of John Cusack movies we'd gone to and he'd chimed in, trying to win us over.

It had worked.

For a while.

Tommy really did like old movies. But mostly he liked telling us that he did.

Paris and I did not tell our not-quite-yet stepfather that Beach Cinema was our place, though. Of all the things Tommy learned about my sister and me in those early days, this was not one of them. I think it felt private—our own safe world where images floated on screens and nice bartenders put cherries in our Cokes and life as it really was seemed far removed for a few hours. It made me think of those castles she used to draw for us.

Once, I told Paris I could live in that movie theater. Not forever, but for a while. Like those kids in that book where they hid out at the big art museum in New York.

"Crazy," Paris had said. But I could tell she was thinking maybe it wasn't. I hadn't thought about all that in a long time. Because who remembers dumb stuff you say when you're a kid? But I was thinking about it now.

"If you're so positive. We'll go there," Max says. "Beach Cinema. Then we'll see."

My stomach pinches. Somehow the way he says it makes me understand that no matter what, there's a time limit to this journey. If we don't find Paris today, soon, we'll drive back to Vegas and whatever this is between us, me and Max, will disappear, fading into the air like smoke from a lit match.

Gone.

It occurs to me now that Tommy Davis is not the only liar I know. I'm one, too. This road trip—no matter how it turns out—isn't enough. I want more than just one kiss on the beach. I want more good things to happen.

To me. To Paris. To Max.

They can, can't they?

I think again about how every atom, every electron is interconnected. Maybe when Max and I kissed, some infinitesimal piece of that kiss touched everything else in the world.

It is a bright and shiny thought, and it sits with me as we use up the hours until Beach Cinema opens at noon.

We find a diner and both order eggs and toast and hash brown potatoes with cheese. We eat. I insist on paying, but Max leaves the tip. We walk around, then go back to the truck and drive down the street of our old apartment building. I point to the second floor, to my bedroom window. I show him where we went to school.

We wander the Promenade and browse and drink more coffee and I tell Max how once out on the sidewalk there was this group demonstrating salsa dancing and Paris joined in and this girl in a red dress with long dark hair taught her the steps and then my sister danced and danced with this short guy who told her he was from Brazil. He twirled her around until Paris was dizzy and breathless and laughing like a maniac.

I remember watching her, knowing as I did that her easy grace would never be mine. Even at thirteen, I could calculate complex math problems and later things like Planck's constant, but Paris—she could dance.

At five minutes past twelve we step inside Beach Cinema. The marquee announces a midnight *Rocky Horror Picture Show* and a marathon of detective movies beginning with *Chinatown*, which I have never seen.

My heart gives a quick surge. Except honestly, what do I expect? To walk in the heavy glass doors and see Paris thundering down the ancient red carpet, grinning at us?

Maybe. Yes.

"You have tickets?" The girl behind the concession stand—twenties, half-sleeve tats, both eyebrows pierced with bars—leans across the counter. She arches her thick eyebrows in a way that is more directive than optional, metal bars waggling. We've skipped right by the ticket window outside.

"Did a tall girl with long hair come in and walk upstairs?" I ask hopefully. "Maybe with a twisty bracelet and some hair clips?"

She responds with a snort and shuffles a giant box of Dots next to a giant box of Milk Duds (worst candy name ever) in the glassed-in shelves at her waist.

Okay then.

"Um," I say. "I used to live around here. We'd come here all the time. He's never been. I wanted to show him the balcony. We'll come right down. I promise." Like Max had earlier, I hold up three fingers in the Boy Scout salute, but this does not seem to impress her. Okay then. Not the scouting type.

The concession-stand girl drums her fingers on the counter. A tiny diamond stud piercing right above her mouth twinkles as she purses her lips.

"Well," she says, looking both bored and annoyed. "If you're not just going up to use the bathroom. They hate when I let people do that."

"Thanks," Max says, smiling sweetly. And then he looks sort of anxious, which surprises me. "I can look around down here while you go up," he says. "You know. Divide and conquer."

"Are you kidding? C'mon." I turn to the girl. "We'll only be a few minutes," I say.

I gallop the red-carpeted stairs two at a time before she can change her mind. Max trails behind, his footsteps slower on the stairs than mine. Old movie posters ascend the stairway walls. A fedora-wearing Humphrey Bogart stares at us from the last poster before we reach the second floor.

I wait at the top step, impatient, for Max to catch up.

"Leo," he says from behind me, voice oddly stiff.

Only I'm not paying attention to that so much because I'm eyeing the older guy behind the bar. The one with the ponytail and the tie-dyed shirt and the bird tattoo on his neck, wings spread like it's trying to take flight.

"Oscar?" I say, voice rising in a question even though I'm sure it's him. I can see the tray of drink condiments that he's probably just filled since they've only been open a few minutes. A huge pile of those maraschino cherries sits smack in the middle of the sectioned tray.

He looks up. A grin spreads across his face.

"Leo? Leo Hollings?" He steps around the bar, recognition growing in his eyes.

At first this throws me. I didn't expect him to remember

after all these years. Then my brain kicks in. Paris must be here! Why else would he know me? My heart thumps to the beat of a country tune.

"Oscar," I say again, testing the waters. "You're looking good."

"Whatcha doing here, Leo?" Oscar says, striding over. "Haven't seen you and your sister in . . . Geez, it's been a while, right?"

I start to respond, stomach sinking, but Max says, "Her sister's here. You sure you haven't seen her?" Something awkward and strange crosses his face.

The back of my neck prickles.

Oscar frowns. "Positive. I remember her, though. Paris. Hard to forget—"

"But she told me—" Max blurts, then stops abruptly, color rising swiftly up his neck, forming bright blotches on his cheeks.

What?

Everything seems to slow, like the room has slid underwater.

Oscar says something I don't hear.

"Max?" I say, my voice loud and screechy and I don't even care. "What's going on?"

"Leo." Max holds out a hand but doesn't touch me. "Leo. Let me explain." His face is pale, his eyes serious and sad.

I feel like I did at the top of the Stratosphere. Breathless and out of control. If I fall, I will land hard and badly and broken.

"Where's my sister?" I squeeze the words out. *Like a black hole,* I think suddenly.

Max steps back, bumping one of the round tables with the rickety metal legs. It topples heavily on the threadbare carpet.

"She's supposed to be here," he says. "She told me she'd be here."

"Told *you?*"

The only explanation is that I'm dreaming. We're still on the beach and I'm asleep, and my brain has conjured a weird nightmare, like the one I had once where I was taking a chemistry test and everyone knew the answers but me.

Max opens his mouth, then closes it, drags out his cell, and gapes at the screen.

He holds up the text for me to see. *Stay in LA with Leo. I'll catch up to you soon. It's almost over. I'll explain then. Tell her to trust you. P.*

"I don't understand," I say, the words sticking in my throat. "Where's Paris?"

"Damn it," he says.

My mind sorts the pieces, slowly, then quicker. I swallow, feeling sick, a terrible fear gripping me as I stare at the tiny words on the tiny screen.

I force my gaze to Max, this boy who has told me about Ashley and made my heart break for him. The one who's driven me around Vegas and then here to California to this place that has stayed in my memory as wonderful and pure. Max who I have kissed. Max who didn't know us before I handed him that piece of pie.

At least that's what I thought.

"I made a mistake," I say.

"Is something wrong with your sister?" Oscar asks.

"Leo," Max says, but I don't want him to talk.

The terrible fear is snaking through my veins, but now anger rushes in, too, clearing my mind, giving me focus.

"What is this? Some kind of sick joke? You don't know her. You barely . . ." I stop then, the thought of what I need to ask forming but not moving because once I let it out, I will have to hear the answer.

"Just tell me, Max." Max who made me trust him. Max who bought a ridiculous pine tree air freshener because I'd complained about his stinky truck. Max who knew physics and was nice to Noah the day camper. Max who kissed me like I'd always dreamed of being kissed.

The Paris and Leo dolls are still in my pocket and now I yank them out, squeezing them in my palm, cutting into my skin. I'm furious—and panicked and humiliated and a million other awful things.

I force myself to give the fear words.

"Did you know Paris before two nights ago at the Heartbreak? When I brought you that piece of pie because she dared me, did you already know who she was?"

"Let me—"

"Yes or no, Max. Had you already met Paris?"

Silence.

"Yes or no?"

"Yes," Max says quietly. "Yes."

I slam the dolls to the floor.

"Leo," Max says.

"No," I say. "No. No. No."

I turn.

I run.

SIXTEEN

MY SIDES ACHE AND I'M GASPING FOR BREATH, BUT I DON'T STOP running. I can't.

Max's hoodie is flopping against my legs, and I wiggle out of it, let it drop in my wake.

The sun is warm and the seagulls are squawking and only the tiniest wisps of white clouds flutter overhead. The ocean smells like where I want to be—far away in some exotic place where terrible things don't happen.

Not to the beach this time, but down the street and onto the wooden planks of the pier, past the welcome sign and the one that reads Route 66. The highway that crosses the country and dead ends here. Unless you dive in and swim, it's as far as you can go.

Not far enough.

Max follows. He might have been a high school athlete,

but he's got loud footsteps and I hear him behind me most of the way.

"Let me explain," he says, the sound of his attempted confession following me like an echo. Now and then he yells my name, and once I shout over my shoulder that he should drop dead, which he doesn't because I keep hearing him.

In New York, a cop might have stopped us, but this is California. People look around for the video cameras like maybe we're filming a movie. So I run faster, chest heaving, stopping only as I clatter by the Ferris wheel—the one that all the tourists go to. The one you see in every movie about LA. I stop short. My breath catches as the wheel moves up and over, up and over—and then stops. I can't help myself. My gaze fixes on the top car. Even from here, I can see it's a guy and girl. Their car starts rocking back and forth—lightly and then more forcefully.

Don't do that, I almost shout, everything inside me wild and out of control.

Me. Who never used to be afraid of heights until the day at the stupid Arizona State Fair. I feel that nauseous, helpless fear.

Everything is falling apart, breaking. Including me.

"Please stop," pants Max, next to me now, out of breath, his hoodie scrunched in one hand.

"Where is she?" I shout it at him.

Max bends at the waist, his hands on his hips. "You're damn fast," he says. "And I don't know. Really, Leo. She was supposed to be here. But she's not. And this is new, anyway. It was her texts I kept answering. I—she was going to be at the Stratosphere. You and I would ride the Big Shot and when we got off, she'd be waiting. That's what we'd agreed on when I said I'd drive around with you. But she changed the plan. Added another note. California, she said. And I figured okay. Why not?"

Why not? I have driven to California with him because of *why not?*

He shoves a hand through his already wildly messy hair. There's a smudge of dirt on his chin. He smells sweaty.

"Call her," I say. "Tell her it's over."

"She isn't answering," Max says. "I don't know where she is."

"Sure you do, Max. She texted your damn phone."

But he shakes his head and says again that he doesn't know. Tells me he deleted my sister's other texts so I wouldn't see them. He talks and talks, and I tell myself he's lying. But I know he isn't. At least not now.

"I trusted you. God, Max."

"She said you needed to get out of your rut." He looks down, blushing red, then redder. "She was going to pay me fifty bucks if I went through with it. I—I thought—"

"Only fifty? Guess that twenty to Nate was a bargain." My own cheeks heat with a humiliation that shoots straight down to my toes. I let him touch me. I *trusted* him. I thought about . . . How could he do this?

"That was before I . . . shit. Leo, you know I'd never . . . Once I knew you, I . . ."

"Gonna finish any of those?" I snap, and he presses his lips together.

In my head I see Max and me on the top floor at the Stratosphere. Feel that Heartbreak receipt in my hands, the one that tallied up what somebody else had eaten. And on the back, scrawled like she was rushing to do something and didn't have time—all those words crossed out—that message about us being happy. The one Max says she added in at the last minute. The one that began the journey that led me here.

"You knew every clue," I say, forcing myself to hold his gaze. "At the Paris, that note on the wall outside. And all the rest of it. Even Beach Cinema. God. I'm such an idiot. Thinking I figured it all out. You must have been having quite the laugh, Max. Poor little Leo. Let's study SAT problems. Let's drive across the desert. Let's pretend she's too sweet and innocent to stay in a hotel room when really you . . . shit. Telling me about you and Ashley. Here's the truth, Max. You were playing me. You and my sister both."

"No. Leo, no. You have to believe me."

Something catches in his voice and I remember how he looked, there on the 108th floor. His jaw tight and his eyes surprised as I read the note. And then stupid Nate said stupid stuff and we went on from there. To the Luxor. To the desert. To the beach.

To here.

I am a stupid girl who makes stupid mistakes and this is what I get.

I don't know what stops me from running again. I want to. Run and run along the beach, hugging the coast until I hit Malibu and then beyond, until I couldn't run anymore. Ventura. Santa Barbara. Whatever.

"I'm going to explain," Max says, no longer phrasing it as a question. "You're going to listen." He reaches out a hand and I slap it away.

"Here's what I think, Max. You want this to even the scales. You help me and it makes up for leaving Ashley. You get to tell yourself how heroic you are."

His face goes pale and tight and I don't care. I can see I've hit a truth. I can see I've hurt him. Good.

"It's not like that," he says. But we both know it is.

He swallows and shoves his hand through his hair a bunch of times and paces back and forth while people side-step around us, some gawking openly, some pretending not to watch our drama unfold.

Let them watch, I think. *Let them see. What difference does any of it make anymore?*

"You've got things *you're* not telling me either," Max says, and my heart stops briefly. "Let's face it, Leo. Your sister is running from something, too, isn't she? I mean, why else . . . I just don't know what it is."

My heart starts up again then, and we holler at each other some more, but everything is lost and wrong and in the end, I don't know what to do except listen to what he has to say.

"Okay," I say finally. "Tell me your side of the story."

What I do not say aloud is that after that I will probably have to call the cops or worse, my mother—whose phone is probably headed toward Hawaii.

I think about her briefly now and the last time we were on the pier—her and me and Paris. It was raining—hard, cold drops, but fresh smelling, mixing with the salt from the ocean and the greasy odor of churros frying. The churro guy was closing up. "This one's on me," he said, leaning into the rain toward my sister. Guys offered her stuff all the time. Mom made us split it in three even bites. I reminded them I had homework.

"He's a good guy," Mom said of Tommy Davis, who we still barely knew. She was in love, she told us. He was the one. Fresh start. New place. Las Vegas! The exclamation mark was hers, not mine.

Now, Max and I catch our breath. Glare at each other. Then we walk the beach again, keeping our distance, threading around sand castles and towels and people enjoying the sun. The sand is warm, the day bright and blue and perfect. California is a sly place, a clever facade.

"You have to understand," Max says. "I first met her about two months ago. She was hanging with some girl who knew someone who knew Nate. At a club in Henderson. There was a poker game in the back and I needed to make some cash so I could pay my rent and that's why I was there. Your sister asked me to buy her a Coke."

I narrow my eyes. "Seriously?"

"Yeah. That's why I paid attention to her. Some girls, when a guy's just won it big, they ask for a beer at least. Your sister asked for a Coke with cherries."

I decide that this time Max is telling the truth.

The rest of Max's story goes like this: They talked. Paris drank her Coke. Maybe they flirted a little. "I hadn't met you yet," he says with that part. Of course he hadn't. I look toward the water, but keep listening.

"I'd see her here and there," he continues, and my mind stutter-steps over his words. "Your sister, well, she's hard to ignore, you know?"

I did know.

"And then I ran into her again a few weeks ago." Max pauses. He glances toward the ocean then back to me, squinting in the bright sunshine. "By then we sort of knew each other. Like you do with people you keep bumping into."

He'd been talking to Ashley's family. Her mom had begged him to come back. Said Ashley missed him and that she wasn't putting her best efforts into her physical therapy. But Max wasn't coming back. Only he didn't know how to say it.

So there was my sister, Paris. The girl who had asked only for Coke. And when she asked for more, Max figured, why not?

"You were right," he tells me quietly. "What you said—before. The way I figured it, if I helped her, helped you, I guess, it would balance things somehow. Erase the debt. Absurd, I know. But that's what I was thinking. She wasn't asking much—just flirt with you and drive you around and follow some crazy clues she'd set up. She said you needed something. You'd been having a hard time. So she'd come up with a plan. And I was the perfect guy to help her."

"God, Max." I make a low hissing sound. Why did Paris tell him those particular things?

Max shrugs. "I asked her why me? You know what she said? 'You have nice eyes. You can trust a boy by his eyes.'"

I heave a noisy sigh. He fell for that?

He reddens again. "I said I knew physics. I never said I was smart."

"You're not," I say meanly. He doesn't disagree.

"So you were fine with all this?" I say, staring him down. To his credit, he does not drop his gaze. "What she was asking of you? Even with you thinking it balanced things. That doesn't . . . You were totally good with it."

My skin feels hot with emotion, the cool breeze drifting off the ocean like an assault to my senses. It had to be more than that for Paris. It had to be. No matter what the truth, there is more to this equation. My sister would not betray me this way. Not now. Not ever.

The heat is back in Max's cheeks but not his voice. "I thought she wanted to hook us up," he says. "Not that I . . .

but when I met you, when you walked over to me with that piece of coconut cream pie—"

He stops walking. His toes crunch at the sand. "You weren't what I expected. When a girl asks you to be nice to her little sister, well . . . you weren't that. And then the more I got to know you, the more I wondered about the whole thing. I'd helped her set up the notes. It felt like a game. It *was* a game. Only when your sister didn't show up like planned, I didn't know what else to do. Then she texted me. Said she'd see us in LA. That was all she'd tell me. She said you'd figure it out. That I needed to let you. That she knew I'd probably think it was crazy but I should do it anyway."

The sun is very bright on his face, gray eyes blinking now and then, his chin scruff fast turning into beard, the prickly hairs lit almost golden.

I turn toward the ocean because looking at him makes my heart contract. I meet a boy I could like, and it's all a sick joke.

Max steps toward me, hair ruffling in the breeze, but he does not reach out. He knows better.

"You're not what I thought," he says again.

"Spinning your wheels, Max," I tell him, and his hands clench, then release. "You don't know me at all."

He asks, "You know what Bose-Einstein condensate is?" and I frown because how random is this?

"I thought you secretly hated science." My nostrils flare

at his now-obvious lie. "Enough with the physics. Joke's over, Max. Give it a rest."

"Just listen," Max says. His voice rises into the salt-tinged air. "You know how things are solids or liquids or gases, right? Well, there's something else, too. A Bose-Einstein condensate—it's different. It's rare. This bunch of particles that usually don't interact—which is lucky for the normal world because if they did, the universe couldn't handle it. In this kind of condensate, the atoms are more like waves—like the ocean. If they ever all came together, they'd form a single giant matter wave. And it would be this hugely powerful thing."

He moves toward me, but I step back, feet pressing the warm sand. Everything around us feels brittle and off balance.

"You're like that," he says, his voice serious. "Like this rare and wild thing. Leo, I . . ." He stares at me, but I look away because I can't hear something like that from him—not now—and then he finishes, "I'm sorry."

"About what?"

He grips my arms, tight and sudden before I can step away again, cinching his hands around them.

"Let go." I tug, pulse going jagged. "Don't."

"Think, Leo. Why would she do this?"

"Get the hell off me."

"Think." He drops his hands. "Why? Why would she want you out of Vegas? Is there something she's afraid of?

There's got to be something, Leo. Think about it."

I kick the sand. "I don't know. Something with her boy-friend, Toby." But that doesn't make sense anymore, does it?

"Maybe. But why would she lie to you?"

"Why would *you*?" I snap, and then feel a tiny bit sorry for it. The question swirls my brain anyway. Because he's right. It has to be something.

When I was little and I was upset, I would add numbers in my head for as far as I could go until I calmed down. Three and five and eight and then I'd repeat it up and up until I lost interest or made a mistake.

I'm not little anymore, but I need to add up the clues that same way.

But I'm not thinking clearly right now. I'm scared and I'm angry. Everything is bubbling inside me, threatening to spill out and over.

I've left you the clues, Paris says in my head. *Not my fault you're so dense, little sister. You need to stop running.*

I know I'm just imagining her voice. I know on some level it makes no sense since all Paris has led me to do is run and drive and move. To disappear like she has. But I am desperate enough to take it seriously.

This isn't only about me, my sister's voice continues. *You know that, Leo.*

"We need to go back to the theater," I say, already walking.

Max doesn't argue, just trails behind.

"This doesn't mean I forgive you," I toss over my shoulder.

Max makes an agreeing sound in the back of his throat.

Oscar is waiting, elbows on the bar, chin in hand, thumbs resting on the bird tat on his neck.

"Figured you'd be back," he says, something uneasy flickering across his face and then disappearing. My Leo and Paris dolls are lying faceup by his elbow. I pick them up, cradling them in one hand.

Oscar asks if I want a Coke with cherries. I do. He spritzes soda in a tall glass. Adds an extra cherry.

"Thank you," I say, and we smile briefly at each other.

Max and I shove two of the little rickety round tables together, pull up two disreputable-looking folding chairs, one with a jagged rip in its pink seat cover.

Oscar sells a large plastic goblet of red wine to some guy in board shorts, sandals, and one of those hats with earflaps. The guy asks him for a straw.

I am grateful that Oscar seems to feel no need for any further explanation. He asks once, "You good, Leo?"

I nod. He watches me for a few beats. Then turns to pour kernels and oil in the small popcorn machine against the wall.

"Let's go over it again," I say to Max, then sip some Coke, spearing a cherry with my straw. "What the hell is she trying to tell me?"

And so we put our heads together, Max Sullivan and me, like two students studying for a test. I don't know what else to do.

We review all of it, every note, every text, every idea and intuition.

The original note on Elvis's leg that started it all gets discussed first.

"She wrote 'he's making me,'" I say, pointing to the words on the note that I've carried all this way in my pocket. "I thought it was a joke at first and then maybe Toby, her boyfriend. And now . . . I don't know."

"Does your sister have enemies?" Max asks, and I shrug and make a face.

"This isn't a movie," I tell him. But my heart beats hard just the same.

The note from the Eiffel Tower leg is next. Nothing much there except that it led us to the Big Shot on top of the Stratosphere.

"That's why I put the money in the slot machine," Max says sheepishly. "To give her time to set it up."

I sigh. He says he's sorry again. I say, "Let's keep thinking." And begin to wonder: Did she drive all this way alone? I guess she must have.

"I don't know," Max says when I ask him. "I didn't think to ask." But he bites his lip and I can see that maybe he wishes he had. Me, too, Max.

We talk about the Stratosphere for a while. Max refers

to Nate as a douche, trying to divert my attention from his own douchiness.

I unfold the receipt from the Heartbreak that she'd written on, tracing my finger over her handwriting. *Near the water,* she'd scrawled. *Where we were happy.*

"You knew she wanted us to go to LA," I say to Max.

He nods, blushing. He has done this so much since he confessed that I'm almost sorry for him. Almost.

"But that's all I knew," he says. "Really, Leo. I swear. I wasn't even totally sure about the theater, but you seemed positive, so by then I figured you were right." He flashes his Boy Scout oath fingers again. I refuse to let myself smile.

Or to acknowledge that the Cali sunshine has added to the sprinkle of freckles dusting his nose. I hate that I still think he's cute.

"I'm sorry, Leo. I can't say it enough."

"No you can't," I say. "Let's just find her." It's the only thing that matters.

A bunch of moviegoers stream up the stairs into the balcony and through the porthole-windowed door into the little theater. I want to follow them. Sink into a fading plush seat and lose myself in a movie. Someone else's problems. Someone else's mystery. Sip my Coke, get one of those giant bags of popcorn with butter and forget all this.

"She wanted to come back here with me so bad," I say, more to myself than Max. "She talked about it all the time. But she knew I had school. And . . . she knew I couldn't.

Not yet. I'd tell her when I got into Stanford. At least then if she went, we'd be in the same state."

An old man in a short-sleeved polo holding a box of Swedish Fish opens the door to the theater and music and dialogue filter out. I hear Jack Nicholson's voice from the movie, but not what he's saying.

Tommy likes Nicholson—at least that's what he told me. One time when Paris and Mom were both out, I watched *The Shining* with him. For a while after that he'd see me and say, "All work and no play makes Jack a dull boy," one of the famous lines from the movie. But after the first time, I didn't think it was funny at all, just sort of sad.

We go over the rest of what we know. The postcard of the Hollywood sign with the name Toby on the back. The Leo and Paris dolls, now resting gently on the scarred table.

Max picks up my doll, grinning at its dorky white cardigan on which my sister had stitched my name. "Cute."

I make a face. "She was telling me something with these. That much I'm sure of." I review it again: How when I looked into the dollhouse—was it just yesterday?—the Paris doll was propped in the rocking chair, facing the four-poster bed that held the Leo doll. And the message Paris had left in the other dollhouse bedroom—the one that urged me to leave. Now. To find my sister.

"What if she needed to take your money?" Max says. "Maybe it wasn't just to get you to come find her."

But for what?

Once again, he shakes his head. Once again, he looks embarrassed and confused.

In physics, you have to read the problem carefully. Develop a mental picture. Identify the known and the unknown quantities. Plot a strategy.

Establish what you don't know.

But how do you know what you don't know when you don't know anything at all?

"If she was so desperate for me to get out of Vegas, then why isn't she here? Why not come with me? If she's in trouble, why not tell me?"

Something cold slithers up my spine. I think about *The Shining* again. About how the wife thought her husband was writing this great novel, but really he was typing that one line over and over on all those pieces of paper. Sometimes that happens, I know. We ignore the warning signs.

What if there was something so bad Paris couldn't say it? Is that possible? But even then, why all this? Why make sure I ended up so many miles away?

Max is looking at me now, something dark and unreadable in his expression.

"Leo," he says slowly, like he's working it out in his head. He's looking at the dolls again, not at me. "When you called me—when I came to get you . . . I'd left a message for Paris already, telling her that I didn't think I could convince you to keep on with the whole scavenger hunt. And she'd told me not to worry, but honestly? I was ready to blow the whole thing off."

Max lifts his gaze, eyes suddenly fierce on mine. "But you *called*. And I thought when I saw you . . . Leo, why did you call again? Why *me*?"

A million answers fill my head. A million possibilities. I can't give voice to any of them.

But he's looking at me, really looking.

"I had a fight with my stepfather," I say carefully. "My mother took his side."

"Did it have something to do with your sister?"

"No."

"You're sure?"

My heart is beating very fast. Coke backwashes in my throat, burning.

"Leo?" Max's voice is a question now. I keep my eyes on Oscar's bird tattoo. Wondering what it would be like to fly free like that.

In my head, I see Paris's room—so uncharacteristically chaotic. So many nights lately when she wasn't sleeping, just crafting jewelry like a maniac, stockpiling necklaces and bracelets. And waking me up in the middle of the night to go driving. To eat pie at the Heartbreak. Because she'd broken up with Tobias. That's what she kept saying. That's what made sense.

At least I thought it did. What did I know about boys, really? Or how it feels to break up with one? When Paris asked me about Buddy Lathrop, I told her he was cheap and a bad kisser. But the truth was that Buddy liked me. He thought I was pretty and he said so. I think now that he meant it, but how would I know? I was not pretty, not inside where it counted. It was easier to tell him to go to hell.

Still, if something else was wrong, Paris would have told me. Or Mom. That's what people do. They ask for help.

Except when they don't.

But if Paris was in trouble, I'd *know*. Wouldn't I?

A memory rises of that day Tommy took us all to the Sugar Factory, him and Mom sipping Purple Passion while Paris and I ate grilled cheese with strawberry jam.

"I like your hair that way," he told my sister, who reached up and fingered her long braid. We were sitting outside at a small four-top near the railing by the street. Tommy's elbow knocked into her water glass, almost spilling it.

"Damn tiny tables," he said, and slurped a big sip from my mother's straw.

When Tommy went to the men's room after all that too-sweet booze, my mother leaned across, eye to eye with my sister. "Don't ruin it for me," she told her.

"Leo, what?" Max sounds far away. He reaches out a hand, but my own hands are clutched together in my lap. The floor feels oddly unsteady and for a second I think earthquake, but the quaking is my own.

My brain offers up a montage of images: Tommy sitting

in the dark in the kitchen. Pressing that fifty-dollar bill into my hand. And later, in my room, telling me my sister is eighteen and she can do what she wants. Acting all concerned about *me* touching her stuff. Asking if Paris was off with some guy.

I clutch the table. It is like being on top of the Ferris wheel, the cart swaying hard, then tipping, nothing to keep me from falling.

Max says something else now, but I'm not listening.

More images: Tommy's finger tracing my arm.

No. Paris. Not Paris. He wouldn't have. She . . .

Nothing happened. We don't need the cops, he said. *Your sister knows how to take care of herself.*

But what if that wasn't true? What if she didn't know she had to?

My mouth and throat go dry. The rip on the filthy pink seat cover scrapes the back of my leg as I push from the chair. The room closes in: Oscar at the bar. The greasy smell of popcorn. The muffled sounds of unintelligible dialogue seeping from the theater. The fading posters of movie stars long dead.

"Tommy," I say, not looking at Max. I can't look at him. I can't . . . "He . . ." My mouth won't form the words.

Max figures it out anyway. Because when I finally lift my gaze, I see the look on his face and I know.

"You think he'd do that? Your stepfather. Would he—"

"She didn't tell me," I say, denying still. "She didn't *tell* me." How long has this been going on? Am I right?

Max makes some kind of motion—to hold me maybe?—but I'm already stumbling down the stairs and he's behind me, saying something and I think Oscar yells my name but everything is loud white noise.

I will *kill* him. In my head, I see it. See Tommy dead.

But I can't be sure until I find Paris. I need to hear it from her.

Why didn't she tell Mom? No matter what, she's still our mother. But I know that answer, too. Knew it when I called Max. When I made my choice and walked out the door. My mother sided with her husband when she screamed at me and sent me to my room. Would she have heard the truth if it was offered?

Maybe trusting Max with me was the only thing Paris could think to do.

Talk to him, she told me. *I dare you.* And then: *He's nice, right? He is.*

She wanted to be sure I liked him. If I liked him I'd trust him. I'd let him help me and when she disappeared, together we'd find her.

But every place I go she's not there.

"We're missing something," Max says, and I stop on the sidewalk, breathing hard.

"No we're not. My stepfather has hurt my sister. He's . . ." I can't say the words. I can't think of him touching her. "I'll kill him." This time I say it aloud. "If he's touched her . . ."

My heart careens from my chest, tumbling toward the ocean.

"Leo," Max says. "It doesn't make sense. If he was . . . doing something to her"—I flinch as he says it—"then even if she wouldn't tell you, wouldn't she come here *with* you? If she was worried about herself and by extension about you, why would she just disappear? Why would she ask me to drive you around and . . ."

He's right. It doesn't add up.

"Think, Leo. I mean, if you're right. I know it's the worst . . . but if you are . . ." He pauses, and I have to force myself to keep looking at him, to keep standing here, because all I want to do is run again.

"Let's say I'm Paris," Max says. "And I can't find the words to tell you what's really wrong—maybe I think you won't even believe me—I just want you out of there, want you in LA because for whatever reason this is where I think you'll be safe or far enough away or whatever. If that's the case, then I'd be here to meet you. We know nothing's stopped her. At least I think we do. So why wouldn't she be here to tell you the real story?"

His words bounce against my frozen brain, not penetrating. A foreign language.

"Stop talking," I tell him, covering my ears. "I don't know."

But he asks again, "Why not?" and an answer begins to surface. It sits sharply in my empty chest, waiting.

I think of my sister, of who she is and how she navigates this life of ours. Drawing castles with princes. Making me tell her stories with happy endings. Even as our mother uprooted us, chasing the better life that always receded, just out of reach. I think Paris believed—still believes—that if you pretend long enough, wish hard enough, close your eyes long enough, the desire becomes truth.

Max is still watching me and waiting. Why? I know he hates himself right now—for leaving Ashley, for deferring college, for all of it. But he got in his truck and drove away and came here to make a life that was something else. I know he thinks he's a coward. But I don't.

But Max isn't like me and Paris. He's on his own.

My sister knew I would come for her. No matter what it took. That's what I do.

But what if I was wrong about that? What if this has always been only about getting *me* here?

What if *that* was the thing my sister wanted to do?

I think about my dollhouse and the way I found the dolls, hers protecting mine.

Exactly how far would my sister go to protect me?

And what exactly did she believe she was protecting me from?

I swallow over the boulder in my throat, working out the rest of it, seeing the parts I should have seen but didn't. Couldn't.

My sister slamming the brakes of our Mazda in the middle of the road. *I'd do anything for you,* she told me. Like our mother, I thought she was being dramatic. Being Paris.

What would she do? And if she's not home and not here, then where the hell is she?

If Max and I are both still in the dark, who would my sister trust to help her?

Her friend Margo? Tobias the boyfriend I've never met and who didn't even take her to the prom? Grammy Marie in Paso Robles who we haven't talked to in months and months?

There is only one person that makes sense. Only one person who is not me that my sister would tell things to. That my sister would go to if she needed help.

And that person is not here in LA. Not anywhere near.

"Max," I say. "I need to go home. Now."

He blinks at me curiously. "Why?"

I look at him impatiently. My body feels already somehow in motion—flying back through the desert to Paris.

"The waitress at the Heartbreak. Maureen," I say. In my head I hear her, feel her arm on mine, pulling me aside, asking me if Max was bothering me. Telling me she'd kick him out if he was. *Just say the word and he's out of here.*

I see those dangly red-stone earrings Paris made for her. The ones she wore like all the time. *She's been through stuff,* I hear my sister say.

There is only one reason my sister would send me to LA without her. So she could do whatever she needed to make sure Tommy Davis didn't hurt me like he has hurt her.

Max looks at me, waiting. I hesitate, then tell him what I'm thinking. We've come too far together. I owe him this much truth. His jaw tightens, his face pale.

"Paris is in Vegas," I say. "I don't think she ever left."

SEVENTEEN

WE DRIVE WITHOUT STOPPING, THE SUN BEATING ABOVE THE TRUCK then lowering behind us as we head east, that tiny white scar over Max's eyebrow periodically reflecting the metallic glint from oncoming cars. Sometimes we don't talk at all, and in those moments I rest my forehead against the passenger window, eyes closed but not sleeping, feeling the desert heat on the other side of the glass.

Just somewhere between California and Las Vegas, the road making whumping sounds under our tires, Max says, "I've done other things I'm not proud of."

"Oh?" I turn from the window.

"Drove my dad's Lexus into our front porch two days after I got my license."

"Seriously?"

"It was raining. I was a goober."

We drive most of another mile before I stop laughing. And the thing is, he looks so sweet and earnest as he says it, and I know he's told me because it's the only thing he can think of that might break the tension or make me feel better or less worried or something.

He does not understand that I can laugh even though none of those things are possible.

"I'm a better driver now, though," he adds.

"Good to know," I tell him. And I smile at him because it seems the right thing to do.

The sun is setting, the Luxor light streaming blue, as we head into Vegas. I call my sister for what feels like the millionth time. "I'm back," I say.

No answer except her voice mail. I am not surprised.

Not long after that, we pull into the parking lot of the Heartbreak Hotel Diner, two nights after we've left. I have not called ahead and asked for Maureen.

"Better to just walk in," Max says, and I agree. Less time for her to make up some lie. I am positive she knows where my sister is.

My heart contracts at the sight of Paris's silver Sharpie message, still on Elvis's pants leg.

I half expect Paris to be at the hostess booth as we walk in, but of course she is not.

Maureen, who usually works the graveyard shift, is also nowhere to be seen.

"I'm Paris's sister. Did she come in today?" I ask the hostess. She's the one who was here the other night, I think— skinny, tall, long brown hair in a messy bun stabbed with a pencil. Blue eye shadow. Her name tag announces that she's CeCe. She shakes her head. Tells me Paris called in sick. I exhale a breath I didn't even know I was holding. A phone call doesn't mean she's here. But it means she's somewhere.

"What about Maureen?" Max asks. "You know when she comes on duty?"

CeCe looks him up and down and then says, "She worked day shift today. And left early." She heaves a disgruntled-sounding sigh, then peers beyond us, clearly done chatting.

"We need her address," Max informs her curtly, and her gaze snaps back to him.

"Dude," CeCe says. "We don't give that out."

"It's important," I say firmly, staring her down.

She lifts a pencil-thin arm like it's a huge effort and brushes a loose strand of hair behind her ear.

On the wall, Elvis and Priscilla stare down at us. "Hound Dog" blares from the speakers. The only other person in the dining room is a geriatric lady in a flowery dress with short puffy elastic sleeves. She's sitting at a front table, loud-slurping a bowl of soup.

She glares at us, then glances disinterestedly around the diner. The old lady keeps slurping soup.

Then she adds, "I haven't seen your sister."

I move so we are nose to nose. Her breath is a mixture

of peppermint and something less fresh.

"I need to find her. Maureen knows where she is. *You* need to tell us where Maureen lives."

She shrugs, unruffled by my closeness. "Saw her the other night. You were here though. I think she came in after you left."

Something this side of relief floods through me. If Paris came back that night then maybe I'm right. She's here in Vegas.

"CeCe." Max's gray eyes are storm clouds. "If you know where Paris Hollings is, you need to tell us."

Maybe it's the way he says it. Maybe it's because he's a guy and some girls do what guys say.

Or that ridiculously, tears start running down my face. We've come so far only to meet another dead end.

More likely it's because the cook stomps out of the kitchen, hollering so loudly about the waitstaff's deplorable lack of work ethic (not his exact words) that Priscilla and Elvis shake on the wall.

"Your sister is at Maureen's." CeCe sighs, and my heart stops for any number of beats. And then she tells us the address.

We walk up the driveway to Waitress Maureen's house, small, run-down, but with a pot of flowers by the front steps. Brilliant purples and yellows and bright pinks spilling everywhere. We move neither fast nor slow but with the steady gait of two people who have been trying to get somewhere for days now and, because they both know science, understand that gravity can bend light and that things are not always where we perceive them to be.

We ring the bell, only the little white plastic piece is cracked and we don't hear any sound, so I bang on the door with my fist.

When nothing happens, just a roadrunner skittering by in the growing dusk, looking tired and hot, I thud the door again, palm open. *Bam. Bam. Bam.*

There is the sound of someone walking and stopping, a heavier footstep than my sister could make.

Maureen is wearing skinny jeans and a black sleeveless T-shirt and she is surprisingly sturdy and fit, something I had never suspected. Her arms are muscled, probably from toting those heavy food trays—all those pie slices and sandwiches. But her hair is down and I can see strands of gray at her part where the color has worn off. Her eyes are puffy underneath.

"Leo," she says, and her voice is firm but kind. "Your sister's gone."

EIGHTEEN

"GONE?" MY PULSE EXPLODES. WE CAME THIS FAR AND SHE'S NOT HERE?

Maureen gestures for us to come inside, but I'm already pushing past her to search. What if she's lying? Everyone else is—or at least has.

Family room: no. Kitchen: no. Max shouts my name, but I'm on the move. Bathroom: no. Bedroom: no. Just a rose-colored comforter and some plastic-framed nature scene prints on the walls. Hotel art. The kind of thing my sister hates.

"She's not here, Leo," Maureen says. She reaches for me, but I dart around her.

"What did she tell you? Where the hell is she?" I race to the next room.

No Paris.

"Let me get you something, Leo," Maureen says when,

eventually, I stop searching. "A Coke, maybe? I've got Dr Pepper. Iced tea?"

Why is she talking about beverages? "She was here, right? We need to find her." I feel the fight seeping out of me. To follow all those clues and be right and be so close and then . . . nothing.

"A Coke," Maureen says again. "It settles the stomach." Max nods like he agrees and because somehow he is standing next to me, I let him squeeze my hand.

In the small kitchen that smells like spray cleaner, I stand stiffly at the counter while Maureen pours Coke from a half-empty two-liter bottle into squat glasses. In her waitress outfit she always looks old. Here in her own house, I see that she's not much older than my mother.

I don't want to drink Coke. I need to find Paris.

"I was wrong," Maureen says, lifting her glass but not drinking. "I'm never wrong, not usually. But your sister, I didn't read her right."

Maureen sets the glass down. "People have a way of hiding the bad shit. I should have paid better attention. But I thought I knew her. I thought—"

"What did Paris say?" My heart is thumping and my brain is parading horrible things.

Max rubs a hand over my shoulders, but I shrug it away.

"Maybe you should sit down," Maureen says. "You don't look so good."

She starts to say something else, but I have no patience.

"What did you mean that you were wrong about Paris?" I blurt. "How long was she here? Did you know that she sent me and Max all the way to LA looking for her? You knew, didn't you? But you let me go. Why would you do that?"

The words tumble out of me, water through a broken dam.

Maureen's brows squinch together. She cocks her head like I'm speaking Swahili. "What? You did what? I just figured . . . you drove to LA? Why the hell would Paris make you do that? She came back after you left. Shit. I had no idea. Leo, honey, I would never . . ."

She interrupts herself with a string of creative swear words. Everything inside me feels combustible and unbalanced. I had convinced myself she knew. But she doesn't.

"She said your mother kicked her out. That they got into a fight over her boyfriend and she needed a place to stay. You know I like Paris. She's a sharp one, your sister. So I said sure. It didn't occur to me that—"

"Fight?" I gape at her, mouth dropping open.

Maureen makes a thick sound in the back of her throat like she's going to spit. "It's bullshit, isn't it?" She twists the cap back on the Coke bottle, but the cap slips from her hand and bounces—a tinny sound—onto the floor, rolling into a corner. "She had this whole story—had me believing she needed out of your house. Said you'd try to make peace with the family because that's how you were and she didn't want that. She wasn't sure what she was going to do.

Wanted to think things over. Just for a day or so, she said. That's why she ran out on you like that."

"She wrote me a note on Elvis's leg. Didn't that seem off to you?"

"Leo," Maureen says. "A guy came in the other night without pants. Nothing seems off to me." But her eyes are serious.

She opens a drawer at the counter, her hands rummaging even while she holds my gaze. "Where are those damn cigarettes?" She seems to direct the question to the drawer. "Try to quit and try to quit, but I never do."

I stare at her, attempting and failing to process, except that Maureen believes things in our life are so horrible she was willing to hide my sister from it.

More rummaging and now Maureen is opening another drawer, then slamming it closed and back to the first. "Damn it," she says.

"You need some help?" Max asks. I'd almost forgotten he was here. Maureen ignores him, yanking the drawer again, this time with such force that it pulls full out of the counter. It drops with a hard thud on the tile floor, spewing papers and coupons and pencils and random clots of junk.

"But it's been two days. And I . . . I came home a little bit ago," she begins, words coming faster now. "Said I had a migraine coming on and left early. I'd been working double shifts and enough is enough sometimes, you know? Your sister—she wasn't expecting me. She was at the table, but I don't think she heard me because she was listening to music and her earbuds were in and she was scribbling on a piece of paper. So I walked over and I see that she's drinking my red wine. I told her she needed to tell me what the deal was. I'd help her if I could. But I didn't need any trouble. I had enough of my own."

My heart pounds its way up my throat and then higher, beating in my ears, my temples.

"Did she tell you anything?" I say, voice very small.

Maureen says, "No."

Max is frowning, looking from Maureen to me to the crap on the floor from the fallen drawer and back through the cycle. Maureen sinks to her knees by the drawer, pawing at it now with her big-knuckled hands, the muscles in her arms flexing as she sifts through the papers, looking for something that's obviously not there.

"Your sister said she'd explain. But it had to be quick. She had somewhere to be." She tilts her head, assessing. She has stopped looking for whatever she's been searching for. "She said she thought she had more time to be sure. But you were coming back. I didn't think to ask her where you'd been. And by the time I changed out of my uniform, she was gone."

Maureen looks up at me more carefully. She rubs her hands on the knees of her jeans. "Leo. Was something bad going on in your house?"

I look away. Max is quiet.

"You have to understand," Maureen says, and some-thing in her tone makes my stomach seize. "I live on my own. People who come into the Heartbreak—they're not always the best quality, you know. And then there's my ex-husband, well . . . I have a gun. It's just me in the house, so I keep it here where I can grab it. If he comes in that door—"

"Gun?" I whip my gaze back to her, to the mess on the floor.

"In the drawer," Maureen says, pointing. "But it's gone. Just like your sister."

"Gun?" Max says. "She took your gun?"

It all makes terrible, horrible sense. Of course Paris would send me away. Not just to keep me safe. But so when she went after him, I wouldn't be there to stop her.

I know then what she plans on doing. And when he looks at me, I know that Max does, too. His fists clench and then unclench. Like he's going into battle for me, and that crazy thought feels like a miracle that will be put to no use.

"She knows I'm here," I say to him. "Because I called her and she knows and now she's got a gun." My voice comes out weirdly calm.

"What the hell does your sister need a gun for?" Maureen's voice rises to the ceiling. She pushes fast off the floor.

"It's not your fault," I say, and I really mean it.

"What's going on here, Leo? That's my fucking gun she took. Shit."

"Leo," Max says quietly, his voice barely audible. "Is there more to this?"

But I'm already running out the door.

NINETEEN

HE CATCHES UP TO ME AT THE TRUCK.

My body is shaking, little nervous tremors, like when there'd be a small earthquake in LA and you might not have even noticed except that the floor felt like it was humming.

I ask Max for his phone, and when he hands it to me, I press in the numbers.

Sure enough, Tommy picks up. The sound of his voice runs up my spine like nails. But he has no way of knowing it's me. He won't recognize Max's phone.

"Who the hell is this? Damn computers keep calling and not saying anything," he says, and in the background I hear slot machines and chips clinking and someone very near the phone asks, does he want to double down? Then there's a shuffling sound and a muffled PA announcement somewhere in the background, and he hangs up.

My heart freezes. This is the first time I've called him since Paris disappeared. Has someone else been trying to pin down his whereabouts?

Paris.

Max waits, key in the ignition. Max who is on the run from his own life and from Ashley Pennington, who loved him. Even if he goes back to Texas, even if he goes back to her. It may never end for him. I get that now. I do.

Some things happen and they're forever.

"Vegas Mike's," I tell him, heart beating way too fast, body numb. "That's where we need to go. That's where he is. That's where she'll go."

Or is going. Or has gone. It could be too late. How could it *not* be too late?

"You sure?" Max cranks the engine. "Lots of casinos out there."

But only one where behind the din, just before each half hour, a voice pops up on the PA: *Vegas Mike's Man Buffet. All-you-can-eat wings and fries and beer, served by our Vegas Mike dancers.*

This is what I heard when my stepfather answered his phone.

If I could figure out where he is, so could my sister.

We drive. More than once I want to say, *"Don't stop. We'll head somewhere else. Back to Cali again. Or east, maybe. Hang out in Phoenix or head up to the mountains. Go somewhere I've never been. Nebraska. Iowa."*

Max aims the Ranger toward an available space, shoving the car into park before it's even fully stopped. "How do you know she'll be here? How do we even know any of what you think is true? Even if it is—why now? Why not while we were on the road?" Max grabs my hand in his and I don't pull away. His palm is rough in the center, like he's scraped it on something. "Leo. Come on. Think about it."

But he sounds unsure.

I know my sister better than anyone. Know her inside out and backward—at least I did.

Now I wonder if we know each other at all.

For the millionth time since all this began, I wonder why Max has stuck with it. I forgive him for his lies. I really do. So he climbs from the truck and I do the same and then we're standing in the parking lot by Vegas Mike's, a sea of cheap neon and sparkle flashing over our heads.

There is so much that I want to say to him. I open my mouth, but nothing comes out.

"Let's do this," Max says, reaching for my hand. I understand now that he, too, is a Bose-Einstein condensate. A rare, amazing thing.

But I race ahead of him instead, feet slapping the asphalt, mouth dry as old leaves, not stopping when he calls my name.

* * *

Vegas Mike's is dim and smoky, and there's a smell of beer and money and sweat. Somehow, my mother senses when I find her. She looks up, cards in her hands, her table filled at every seat. "Leo!" she hollers across the casino, and heads turn as her voice rises over all the other noise. Even from here, I can see she's torn between running to me and staying put like she needs to because she's the dealer and the table is crowded with people and money and chips, red and black and purple and green and blue. Dealers cannot leave their tables. Ever.

I wave, arm overhead, in a gesture that I hope says *stay put*. I am not here to see her, not yet. My eyes drop to the players. None of them is Tommy Davis. But he wouldn't be there anyway. Mom refuses to deal to people she knows.

I scan the floor for my sister. Maybe I'm wrong.

"Leo!" Mom is calling my name again, the pit boss towering behind her, saying something I can't hear, his body language stiff and pissed off.

Again, Max catches up with me. There's a coffee stain on the bottom of the black T-shirt he's been wearing since we left Vegas. The leather ties of one boat shoe have come undone. He's a mess right now, Max Sullivan. But when he looks at me, my heart hums, even as my brain says that there is no good ending on the way.

"I don't see her," he says, craning his neck this way and that. "Do you?"

I look again, scan this small dump of a casino where

waitresses in shorts and skimpy tank tops serve you beer and wings and wear a utility belt of hot sauce choices around their waists so the big tippers can dunk a wing and slip a buck or two in the belt.

Only one room isn't visible from here in the lobby entrance. The high-stakes poker room by the bathrooms, not far from a bank of popular slots.

I'm half running now, not caring if Max follows. If I am going to lose him for real, I want it to happen fast. Like ripping off a Band-Aid, exposing the wound underneath.

Paris. I repeat it in my head, over and over, like a mantra. *Paris. Paris. Paris.* If I say it enough times, then maybe she'll appear. Poof, like in the fairy tales.

What will I do when I see her? What will she do? Will she use Maureen's gun? Is she even here?

And then there's Tommy. The reason we are all here in this place that none of us want to be.

When I see him hunched at a Haywire machine, pressing in his bets, I freeze.

Tommy Davis. My mother's husband. My stepfather. Dressed like always—in jeans and boots and a tight white tee, Camel between his fingertips.

"Leo?" Max says. Which is when I realize he doesn't know and so I say, "Tommy." Then I ask Max for his phone. My hands are shaking so hard, but I press in Paris's number and start to leave a message. "I'm here at Vegas Mike's," I say.

My brain is reeling. Everything is imploding, each dream folding in on itself, collapsing and collapsing, pulling pieces of my heart with it.

I'm still speaking into the phone when my stepfather turns around.

He gets up from the Haywire machine and starts toward me, head cocked and eyes narrowed. That's when I hear her.

"Stay away from her," Paris says, hand in her pocket. She's walked out of the ladies' room. She's wearing jeans and a baggy hoodie I've never seen before and her hair is pulled back, tight, in a single braid. She looks thinner than two days ago and exhausted but otherwise the same.

"No," I say. "Paris. Don't." The hoodie pocket looks heavy, sagging. My heart rockets. Maureen's gun?

But I run to her anyway, leaving Max, ignoring my mother, swerving around my stepfather, whose eyes have that slightly unfocused look from too much time staring at the electronic slots. Something huge is about to happen, but it doesn't matter. The only important thing is Paris.

Her eyes dart from me to Tommy and then to me again.

"You're not supposed to be here," she says, voice soft and pleading. "You're in LA. Why the hell aren't you in LA?" She sees Max then, and her voice catches, just a little. "You said you'd take her. Why didn't you make her stay away?"

I cross the carpet, grabbing for her, ignoring everything else. "Are you okay?" I say, trying to keep my voice steady.

"You should have told me. Why didn't you tell me?"

She shakes her head, gaze sliding back to Tommy. Her hand has not moved from that sagging pocket.

"Tell me," I say. "It'll be okay, Paris. Don't worry. I'm back. I know you. . . . I'm back. I'm here. He's not going to hurt you anymore."

I slide my gaze to Tommy. "How could you?" I say, but I don't think he hears me.

He takes another step, looking from Paris to me and then over my head toward Mom's blackjack table. I do not turn around.

"What the hell are you girls up to?"

I should have known. I should have stayed. I should have figured it out.

Around us, the casino noises continue. People betting and drinking and laughing, the smoky air thick as fog. Someone shouts joyfully as a slot starts ringing.

"He's not going to touch you again," I say. "You don't have to . . . I'm sorry, Paris. I thought because . . . I never would have . . . But I figured it out. . . . Paris, please. Don't."

"You were supposed to stay away," my sister says.

I pull on her arm, but she shakes me off. "Let's go," I say. "We'll go somewhere. Wherever you want. Don't look at him. Just look at me."

But my own gaze returns to Tommy anyway. Locks in and holds there. For one small second, I think I see fear.

"Leo?" Max is on the other side of me now.

"I don't want you here, Max," I say. "You can't be here anymore." I know none of this makes any sense to him.

My sister turns to face our stepfather.

"I want you out of our house," Paris says, voice like ice, but she reaches her free hand and somehow, without looking, finds mine. "You are not going to come near us ever again."

"What's this about, Leo?" Tommy steps toward us. A muscle ticks in his thin jaw. His eyes are dark and wide. He doesn't think I'll say it. Why would I now?

"It's okay, Leo." Paris tightens her grip on my hand, but does not remove whatever is in her pocket.

The fear inside me pulses stronger, making my fingers feel numb.

"C'mon," I tell her, voice cracking. "We can't stay here."

"Paris," Max says. "Let your sister help you. She knows what you asked me to do. It's over now. Whatever . . . You don't have to . . . It'll be okay."

"Shut up, Max," Paris says, tightening her grip on me again. I tug to free myself, but my sister is very strong.

A Vegas Mike girl appears as if out of nowhere, beelining to Tommy, a tray of wings and fries and two beers in her hands.

"Got your order, T," she says, smiling, her ass tight in her tiny shorts, boobs spilling from the low cut-tank. "Extra spicy. Miller draft." She offers the food to him, but Tommy

JOY PREBLE

doesn't take it, which seems to throw her.

"Go back to the kitchen, Crystal." This voice belongs to my mother, advancing fast, high heels digging into the cheap carpet. She has either left her table or the pit boss has let her leave, but either way here she is, joining the party. Her face is pale under her makeup, which includes so much mascara that even with all this going on I find myself wondering how she will ever get it off.

"But he ordered it, didn't you, T?"

"And I'm un-ordering it," my mother says tightly. "Go. Now."

"Tommy's leaving, Mom," Paris says. "Just so you know. He's packing up as soon as he walks out of here and he's getting the fuck out of our house and he's not coming back."

Mom's mouth opens and shuts, a fish on a line. "What the hell are you talking about? Where have you been? Both of you?" She looks at Tommy briefly, but her eyes settle on Max. "What have you gotten my girls into?"

"Ms. Hollings," Max says slowly. "You need to ask Paris. She needs to tell you what's been going on."

"Leo," Paris says. She is still holding my hand, looser now, a casual hold, like we are about to skip down the street. Her voice is gentle and that scares me more. Her hoodie pocket is still sagging with what I know is Maureen's gun.

"Leo," Tommy Davis says, voice soft, but I hear something sharp underneath. "What's going on here with you two? Your mother's been worried sick." He holds his hands

236

up like he did the other night in Paris's room.

I want to be on the beach again, the Pacific stretching out blue and endless, churros frying in that little stand up on the pier, the white statue of Saint Monica waiting for me on the street.

With a swiftness that takes me by surprise, my sister places both hands gently on either side of my face. She leans in. Her eyes are dark, and against my skin the side of her thumb feels ragged, like she's been chewing on it. This does not make her any less beautiful. Paris Hollings, my strange and fragile and wonderful sister.

"I'm sorry," I say, because my absence in so many ways has betrayed her, but she shakes her head.

"Leo," Paris says, her voice a whisper. "You need to listen. He never touched me. But you're back here now and you need to tell the truth. You need to say it."

I stand very, very still. The noise and people and even the Texas Tina machine playing a tinny loud country song that absurdly reminds me of Max fade away. It is just me and Paris.

I try to look away. She holds me tight. "The truth, Leo," she says quietly. Gently. And then she lets me go.

I don't want to look at Max's face, but I see it anyway—watch the understanding flicker like a candle barely lit and then burning—and I look away.

Because how could he not know, really? I've been telling him in one way or the other since we left Vegas.

I contemplate running, but that's all I've been doing. The panic has filled every piece of me. In my head I see the ocean again, vast and deep and unknowable. I imagine it covering me, sinking below the surface. But I think now it would only spit me out on the sand, naked and exposed.

That's the thing with secrets. Eventually, something pries them loose for everyone to see.

Mom is staring at Tommy. The one who brought us here to the desert where nothing has ever been the same. "What's going on?" she asks, directing this not to us but to him.

My mother is many things—not all of them good—but in the end, she is just like the rest of us, wanting to believe that everything will turn out okay.

"It has to stop," Paris says.

There's a crowd now, but not a big one. There are many distractions in Vegas Mike's. We are just a small group of people clumped together, talking, and a waitress still standing with us, extra-spicy wings on her tray going cold.

"Leo," Max says. He has a way of saying my name that I could learn to like, but this will probably be the last time he says it.

"Just do it," I tell Paris, wanting it over. "Please."

I am not sure what it is I want her to do. Or if I am, the words don't come. I just want it over.

She looks at me, tears in her eyes. "No," she says.

"That's why you came here," I tell her.

"No," she says.

"Paris," my mother says. "Has someone hurt you?" She can't say the rest of it, but I see it in her eyes.

Tommy edges toward me. Or maybe he's edging away from my mother. I don't want to look at him, but he won't drop his gaze and so I stand frozen, the truth too big and too awful and I can't. I just can't.

He keeps on closing the distance. I suppose that's all he can think to do.

Paris reaches back into her sagging pocket. The entire world has burrowed into my lungs, heaving in and out.

And then there is Max stepping between us, his body in front of mine, one arm stretched to press against me. To protect me.

"Get away from her," he says to Tommy. His arm stays pressed against me, firm and warm. A gift I do not deserve.

This is why I finally end it.

"Paris," Mom says again, not looking anywhere else. "Has Tommy hurt you?" She skirts around it still, but we all know what she means.

"No," I say, breaking. "Not Paris. Me."

"Liar," Tommy says, his voice furious, but now I can hear the fear in his voice. In my head I see him, and the times he's come into my room.

Not Paris. Not Paris. Me.

TWENTY

THE FIRST TIME, ALL I KEPT THINKING WAS: THIS ISN'T HAPPENING. NOT in our house. Not to me.

When he was done, he said, "You can't tell your mother," zipping himself back up. "You know she won't believe you, Leo. This stays between you and me."

The panic rose so fast, I almost threw up.

I lay there as he left my room, knocking into Tiny Tim on his way out. The skeleton—the one I'd showed him so proudly that day we moved in—crashed to the floor. I cradled it in the dark for the rest of the night, both of us broken.

And when he came back, I had no idea how to stop him. Because if I stopped him I had to tell. And how could I tell this? Even to Paris, to whom I had told mostly everything in my life. Paris, who needed the world pretty and perfect.

I was the strong one. That's how it worked between us.

The last time, I nicked my arm on my nightstand, trying to push him off. That was the cut Paris had seen. Somehow she knew. Finally, she knew.

And then she saved me.

Max stands a distance away, watching, shoving his hands through his hair like this will make it all go away. His gaze never leaves me, but after a while, I don't look at him anymore because it makes me too sad. But I know when he walks over to Paris, stepping close, letting her hand him the gun, which he tucks into his waistband under his shirt. I don't know what he does with it after that.

Lots of things happen then: yelling and denial and my mother cries a lot and she slaps Tommy Davis across the face, hard, the side of her wedding ring nicking his cheek and drawing blood. He presses a hand to his face, and I see the tattoo of my mother's name still etched on his wrist.

Then casino security. Then the cops.

Somewhere in all this, Max leaves. There is no gun for anyone to find. Paris denies there ever was one. For now, that part is dropped. There is enough for the cops to do.

"You're telling the truth?" Mom asks me like a million times, and eventually I turn away from her, too.

I ride with my sister and mother in the back of a squad car to the police station on Tropicana. We file charges and talk about restraining orders. I sit in the chair and the lady cop asks me questions and brings me coffee and a dough-nut as though these things will help.

I force myself to look at Tommy Davis as another cop walks him by to a separate room. If he feels me staring, he does not turn around.

My mother cries a bunch and asks again, her voice high and shrill, if I am telling the truth. At some point Paris screams at her to shut up. She keeps crying.

Eventually, that part is over.

I tell Paris that I want to stay at Maureen's. It is not the strangest choice, not really. I cannot go back into our house until I am sure that Tommy is gone forever and right now that hasn't happened. He is, after all, still married to our mother. And as he somehow had a lawyer and it is his word against mine, the police have let him go, at least for now.

More arguing.

But I get my way and so somewhere around two in the morning, Paris drives me—reunited with my phone and money—to Maureen's little house with its bright pot of flowers on the steps. She's agreed to take me in.

"I want to stay, too," Paris says when we arrive.

"Of course," Maureen says. And for whatever reason, I think of that white saint statue on the beach.

After some more crying and arguing and the moment when I tell my mother that I hate her even though I prob-ably don't, Paris and I move ourselves temporarily into

Waitress Maureen's spare bedroom until we can find a place of our own. I will not live with my mother again for a very long time. Maybe never.

Only once we've unpacked the few belongings we've taken with us does the thought occur: I will never walk the beach at Santa Monica with my mother again. Of all the things that have been lost to me, of all the things like medical school that I might never achieve, this one somehow feels among the worst.

But I also know this: I will also never be my mother, at least not the bad parts, the piece of her that wanted to be taken care of so desperately she let it ruin her.

I remember what I told Max as we stood in the middle of nowhere, leaning against his truck and he tried to make me understand how worthless he felt. Did I mean the words I told him then? There is no way to know. But I think about them now anyway. How we are all made of stardust. From the ones that burned the brightest. They live on in us.

Destruction isn't permanent. At least that's what I tell myself. If it's a lie, I'm good with it.

I will hold on to that, too.

Sometime later, Paris and I sit on the bed in our temporary room, the sun just barely rising outside, desert heat already warming the window. Maureen has unearthed half a leftover pie from her refrigerator. We're eating chocolate cream with plastic forks.

Our voices are hoarse from talking, from telling each other the missing parts. We talk until there is nothing left to tell. Just us, this tiny room, and a piece of Heartbreak's famous pie.

The truth, I think now, is like the ocean—always moving, rolling at us and then rushing away.

"You're going to be everything that's good," my sister says in between delicate bites.

"I'm not," I say, voice small.

"You are," she insists, and I leave the words alone, sitting between us, as overly sweet as the pie. Her brightly colored nails, I see now, are chipping here and there.

"I came back for you," I tell her then. "I would always come back for you."

"I know you, Leonora," Paris says, looking down and then at me. "Inside and out, right?"

She ruffles my dirty hair. Her gaze moves to the paper plate, and she smashes the last scrap of pie with her fork, cream filling oozing through the thin plastic tines.

When she looks at me again, she's crying, tears dotting her lashes.

"Don't," I say.

So she doesn't, just leans across the empty pie plate and pulls me into a hug.

"I kept waiting for you to say something had happened. But you wouldn't. Not a word. So I kept telling myself I was wrong. That he was just a jerk, like that time—I bet you don't even remember—on the Ferris wheel at that stupid Arizona State Fair. While Mom was waiting in that idiotic line to buy that pineapple freeze thing she had to have. When he rocked the damn car over and over just to scare us or whatever."

"I remember," I say.

She hugs me again, a quick squeeze of my shoulders. I think briefly of Max, then remind myself that he was just temporary and concentrate on the way my sister's two lower front teeth overlap just the tiniest bit.

Would she have really shot Tommy? What then? If Max hadn't been there, would I have let her? I don't believe I would—even if inside I wished it. But I think about it anyway: Is that why I called her when we were nearing Vegas? Not that I had known about Maureen's gun then. Only that my sister—who had created castles and princes with blue hair and crazy games to make the world bearable— would do *something*. Anything.

While all I could do was run.

That is part of my truth as well.

I understand now what my sister has done to save me: sent me on the road in order to keep me safe. I know what the prize was in this crazy scavenger hunt. Me. Like those faces from the pictures in that red wallet, my sister, Paris, believed she was taking the ugly pieces of my life and turning them into a pretty riddle for me to solve. That is all that matters.

"What about Toby?" I ask her. "You wrote his name on that Hollywood postcard."

My sister scrunches her nose. "Who would date a boy named Toby?"

I shake my head. Decide not to pursue this remarkable piece of my sister's logic.

"And Max?" My heart contracts as I say his name.

"Max was a last-minute addition." Paris hesitates, twisting her ponytail around one long finger.

We both contemplate the wonder of that. And then, like so many things, I choose to let it go. Like the image of Max Sullivan in my head, hands on the wheel, driving us through the desert. Before we came back. Before he knew the truth about me.

I did not know until now that you could grieve the loss of something before you really had it. A Max-shaped hole in my heart.

"Plus he had nice eyes," my sister reminds me, and I can see she really means it.

Paris is crying again, tears welling and then spilling over. "I'm so sorry, Leo."

"Don't," I say, reaching up a hand.

We hold each other tight—two sisters tucked safe as treasures in the borrowed bedroom of an employee of the Heartbreak Hotel Diner. Through the thin walls, I hear the shower and Maureen singing "Suspicious Minds," one of Elvis's favorites.

I will not mourn the loss of Max Sullivan any more than the other things I have lost. That will be my victory.

Max, who I trusted because if a random stranger was good, then so was I. This was what I told myself as we raced through Vegas and then drove through the night.

"You're going to see Max again, right?" Paris whispers in my ear. My sister is still a fan of a happy ending.

We leave it there for now.

TWENTY-ONE

TWO WEEKS BEFORE SCHOOL STARTS AGAIN IN LATE AUGUST, MAXWELL
Sullivan appears as I am constructing a yogurt parfait for a
customer at Yogiberry. I have just swirled the chocolate-and-
vanilla combo into the tall plastic cup and am adding mixed
nuts when he walks in the door and stands at the counter, in
front of the topping choices.

My heart skips a beat, then dances—salsa style.

"You talking to me yet?" he asks.

He has called every day, his messages piling up, unan-
swered.

I shrug, go back to finishing the parfait.

Max folds himself into an orange plastic seat at a table
by the window. He sits and watches me work.

I don't tell him to leave, but I don't tell him anything
else, either. I wring my hands on my apron, below the

counter where he can't see.

He comes back the next day. And the next. I study his expression, finding nothing, but still I know. It isn't the same now. How could it be? I am not the same. I never was.

But he keeps coming back. That has to mean something.

"So," I say to him on the third day, voice casual, pulse skyrocketing. I am arranging blueberries into a cup of peanut butter yogurt. "Did you quit your job? Get fired? Just enjoy stalking me?"

But I'm smiling by day three and when Max stands and walks over, I smile some more even though I don't know what to make of Max, who has now watched me serve yogurt for three days in a row and has even bought a raspberry-and-lemon combo, but only because my douche of a manager kept giving him dirty looks and I still need this job.

"You changed your hair," he says, eyes firm on mine. "I like it." He means the new red streak.

"Purple is so yesterday," I say, tucking a round, thin hazelnut cookie behind the peak of yogurt and blueberries like a fan.

"I want to be with you, Leo Leonora," Max says.

My heart thunders in my chest. I spritz whipped cream on the peanut butter yogurt.

"Leo," Max says. Max Sullivan still enjoys saying my name. "You can't keep not talking to me."

I hand the peanut butter yogurt to the little girl who's waiting, and then, wiping my hands on my pink Yogiberry apron, walk around from the counter.

Max and I stand facing each other but not touching.

What does he see now that he knows the truth? Does he see *me*? Do I want him to? Telling the truth means keeping the truth. Some days it hurts more than I can bear.

Some days—today—I fashion frozen yogurt desserts. It is something, anyway.

"You don't have to do this," I tell him. "You don't owe me anything."

"Leo," Max says. "It's not about that. It's about you and me."

"There is no you and me, Max."

He says, "But there could be."

I listen carefully to his voice, his words threading my heart, my eyes studying his face for hints.

But he says again, "There could be," and adds, "Leo."

It is both my name and the possibility that crack my frozen heart and set it free, bouncing around the yogurt spigots and skating through the topping choices.

We step toward each other, close and then closer, and then right there in Yogiberry we are together, arms wrapping around each other, holding tight. I bury my face against his collarbone, blushing. He smells like lemons and sunshine and warm skin. Someone applauds—possibly the girl with the peanut butter yogurt—but I don't see because Max dips his head and kisses me, soft lips pressing hard against mine.

Tiny specks of nerves bubble, but I rest my hands against the broad and muscled expanse of his back and I am not afraid.

"You kept coming back," I say against his mouth.

"Stardust," he says. "Like you told me."

And then I am crying and kissing him at the same time. How do I explain what Max makes me feel? That there is something hopeful and good in the world. That I am not broken. I want this moment to last forever—except for the Yogiberry shirt and apron. Maybe it will.

A pattering sound at the windows finally pulls me from Max's lips. The sky rumbles. Tiny drops and then bigger, steam rising from the black parking lot asphalt. The storm fades as quickly as it appears, but here in the desert, just for a moment, it's finally raining.

TWENTY-TWO

THE NEXT DAY, SITTING TOGETHER AT THE HEARTBREAK, WATCHING Maureen tote pie and Paris fake politeness to the various customers she's escorting to their tables, Max asks if I will go on another road trip. This time it is for him.

"I need to go to Texas," he tells me. "I want to see my family. I need to set things right."

He does not say Ashley Pennington's name, but I know he means her, too, and this is okay. Like patting Saint Monica's feet even if there is no hope that she can grant what your heart desires, there are just some things that need doing.

"Not for good," he tells me. "I'm not done with Vegas quite yet."

I don't push for more than that.

Instead I tell him that I will come with him, but on one condition—that he helps me study some more for that SAT retake. They've let me reschedule for the September one.

"That's it?" he asks, grinning.

"You're good with probability," I say, not wanting to make a big deal of it.

His smile amps up the wattage. I am almost blinded by it. In a good way.

"If that's what you want," he says, giving in.

I confirm that it is.

Of course we both know nothing is easy—not everyone gets a different life from what they have.

"I got into Arizona State," I tell him casually, like it, too, is no big deal. "They have rolling admission. And a good premed program." Then I tell him that I'm working on my Stanford application.

He drags me from the booth, lifts me, and swings me around the slick tiled floor until I'm giddy with laughter. Elvis and Priscilla are probably laughing, too.

Together, we twirl and twirl. I think of Paris and that day she danced on the Promenade. Will it last—me and Max? I have no earthly idea. But I dance with him now anyway, spin until we are both breathless and dizzy.

"One more thing," I say when finally he sets me down. "For the road trip."

Max looks at me, waiting, curious.

"Paris, Texas," I tell him. "I don't see how we can avoid it. I mean, it seems only fitting, right?"

Max shakes his head. But in the end, he agrees.

* * *

Sitting in the spare bedroom at Maureen's, Max and I plot out our course.

We decide that we will stay overnight in Amarillo and then drive on from there. "Two rooms," I say, giving myself options.

"Two rooms," Max agrees.

And then it will be on to Paris and after that, we'll head south to Houston.

I point to the map on Max's laptop monitor, touch my finger to the tiny black dot of a city that shares my sister's name.

I know this doesn't change things. But the grief, a heavy stone, lifts just a little.

TWENTY-THREE

SO WE HEAD EAST. I NAVIGATE US ACROSS NEVADA INTO ARIZONA, skirting near the Grand Canyon, north of Phoenix, where we'll stop on the way back so I can see ASU, then climbing altitude toward Flagstaff, seven thousand feet up, far from the desert. A brief stop in Winslow—I sing Max an old Eagles song because it's in the lyrics. We drive to my iPod playlists this time, but I've tried to be thematic. Max does not complain. We head into New Mexico, stopping for gas in Gallup, where we gallop around the gas pumps like maniacs on imaginary horses in a very lame play on words, and then continue on to Texas.

In Amarillo, it is very late when we pull in, only one room available, not two. "We can keep driving," Max says. "Or go find that Cadillac Ranch place. Buncha Caddies buried nose down. You have to see it, Leo."

But I tell him it is okay. My heart bumps around and I tell it to calm down.

The motel has a Texas-shaped sink. This prompts a debate about whether all states have this. If we drove to a Motel 6 in Des Moines, would the sinks be shaped like Iowa? The room smells funky, like the AC is leaking somewhere even though everything looks dry.

We lie on the bed, two travelers, and try to sleep.

"You're beautiful," Max whispers more than once, stroking my hair, my face.

And when this makes me cry, both from sadness and fury, he holds me gently and tells me that it will be okay even though we both know that it won't—not for a long time and maybe not ever.

Max falls asleep long before I do. I listen to his slow and even breathing. Once, I see him smile in his sleep, a small curving of his lips. Something like happiness fills me. He stirs, eyes fluttering open. "I can sleep on the floor," he says, almost reflexively.

"You're fine," I say.

And although it is a lie of sorts, at least for now, so am I.

In the morning we dip south through Wichita Falls, then detouring past Dallas so I can say I've been there, listening to my endless supply of Texas songs—"So many," I tell Max, who responds by singing "Deep in the Heart of Texas" in a loud, off-key bellow—and then up to Paris, passing little towns and big towns and huge swaths of nothing but land and trees and grass and heat.

And then suddenly, there it is as we bounce down a road off the main drag. The Eiffel Tower of Paris, Texas. Yet another copy of the real thing, a whole lot shorter, but tall enough. Complete with a ridiculous and massive red cowboy hat perched on top. Above it, the sky—a piercing, cloudless blue.

I am scared. But a plan is a plan. There is no more Tommy Davis rocking the car of the Ferris wheel. There is only me. I tell myself that I am moving forward.

We step out of the truck and the wall of heat hits us. Impossibly, it is hotter in Texas than even Vegas. I hop from one foot to the other because I have forgotten to put my shoes back on and the cement path is scorching under my feet.

Max Sullivan lifts me up and carries me the rest of the way to the fake Eiffel Tower.

He settles me safely on the cooler grass and goes back for my shoes.

When he has slipped them onto my feet, we disobey the warning sign and climb. No one runs out from the community center to stop us. Our eyes meet for a short moment, and then we begin. Max goes first. I follow.

Three very tall rungs up, I freeze, panicked.

"I can't," I say through clenched teeth.

I stand very still, perched on the metal rung, looking at

JOY PREBLE

Max's legs above me. The world reduces to this moment: the beating sun. This idiotic tower with its cowboy hat. The existence of a Paris devoid of anything French. Another road trip with an unknown ending.

Max waits me out. Reminds me to breathe. I think of that day at the Stratosphere. How he held me and breathed with me and for a few small seconds made me believe that everything would work out.

Like his physics hero Albert Einstein, who once famously observed, "The most incomprehensible thing about the universe is that it is comprehensible."

"Just do what I do," Max says. "It will be okay."

I don't believe that, not exactly, but as he also reminds me, we're already three rungs up. It's hotter than hell out here. We might as well keep climbing.

I tighten my grip, the sweltering Texas air thick as soup in my nostrils. My gaze fixes on a clump of trees in the distance. A tiny breeze, barely more than a flutter, tickles the back of my neck.

Out on the road beyond the trees, a pickup truck lumbers by, dust rising in its wake.

"Ready," I say finally, and once more, we start to climb.

It's a messy business—angled rods of metal in between the straighter rungs—and it takes a very long time to shimmy this way and that, and more than once I say I'm giving up but I don't. Eventually, we haul ourselves to a tiny balcony not quite at the top but close enough and just underneath the red cowboy hat. We stand there, out of breath and sweating profusely in the heat.

"We made it, Leo Leonora," Max says.

"That we did," I agree. I steady myself and look around at the whole lot of nothing one can see from up here.

Max looks too, with those ordinary gray eyes that maybe aren't so ordinary after all. Max, who had asked me if I had ever failed big, thinking he was the only one, that his mistakes were worse than anything horrible I could imagine.

In that moment, I understand that it hasn't been the height I'm afraid of, but only the possibility of falling.

"I've got you," Max says, holding my waist.

And then we begin our descent.

ACKNOWLEDGMENTS

Finding Paris is fiction, but girls like Leo and Paris are not. I've known many of them in the classroom, girls whose home lives aren't safe, who may have no way to leave the situation, who struggle to tell their truths, and in part I wrote this book to help give them a voice. As Leo says near the end, "Not everyone gets a different life from the one they have." I think Leo would also say that we all have secrets and pain and things we hide—that we all have a Paris to find. From that place came this novel—part sibling story, part mystery, part road trip, part romance, part exploration of the lengths we go for the people we love.

And now to the thank-yous:

I am forever in the debt of my phenomenal editor, Alessandra Balzer, for loving this story as much as I do, and for her firm direction and endless patience in allowing me the time and encouragement to get it right.

And to the rest of the team at Balzer and Bray, including Kelsey Murphy and copy editors Alexei Esikoff and

Veronica Ambrose, kudos for your eagle eyes and endless references to the cruel taskmaster known as the *Chicago Manual of Style*! Leo and Paris and Max encounter a lot of weird stuff in Vegas and beyond (Eiffel Towers! Giant thermometers!) and they looked up every bit of it to make sure I was getting it right. Which mostly I was.

Although she has moved on to her own new publishing journey since we began this project, hugs to editor Sara Sargent for her early love of the book!

Bravo and cheers to Sarah Kaufman for an amazing and perfect book jacket. Every element is exactly right and when I first saw the cover, I wanted to clutch it to my chest and dance around the room.

I am very, very lucky to be represented by the tireless and brilliant Jennifer Rofé, who fought for this book to find the best of homes and who has been my business partner and cheerleader and friend through the crazy adventure known as publishing. She is one tough cookie, and her Starbucks ordering habits are a frightening thing of beauty. She is also an all-service agent, who even drove one of Max and Leo's road trips and took pictures. Yeah. She's that kind of girl.

The hugest of thanks to my compadres at the Lodge of Death, who heard the earliest snippets of this book when I outlined it one hot Texas summer weekend, surrounded by nature and terrifyingly excessive taxidermy. In particular, my deepest gratitude to Kari Anne Holt, Nikki Loftin, Salima Alikhan, PJ Hoover, Stephanie Pellegrin,

Jenny Moss, Cory Oakes, Jo Whittemore, and Jessica Lee Anderson, who believed in this story from the beginning and insisted that this was "the one."

And to Bethany Hegedus and everyone (including my road trip buddy Christina Mandelski) at the Writing Barn workshop on emotional pacing taught by the very gifted Sara Zarr—thank you for your thoughtful and tough critiques. You helped make this book shine, and I am forever grateful.

To my Houston writing community, critique partners, SCBWI folk, writing partners, and fellow YA Houston members (YAHOO!), thank you for your endless support and for listening when I needed someone to listen. I am infinitely fortunate that there are too many of you to name, but I hope you know who you are and I owe you many plates of gooey Empire Café cake.

And to the Texas bloggers and librarians and booksellers who continue to support me and my career, including but not limited to the staffs of Blue Willow Bookshop, Murder by the Book, and Book Spot, thank you, thank you, thank you!

Finally, to Rick (who vetted every poker scene!) and Jake and Kellie—I love you bunches and bunches and bunches.